Blood for Blood

When Will Grafton's wife is gunned down in a bungled robbery, the middle-aged grocer vows to bring the killers to justice. Grafton hasn't always been a grocer and, as he pursues the ruthless Vallence Gang, it soon becomes clear that the odds are not as unevenly stacked as might at first have been thought.

From the quiet California town of Alila, Grafton's quest leads him inexorably to a bloody showdown in Kansas – a fight from which only one man can emerge alive.

Blood for Blood

Jack Tregarth

A Black Horse Western

ROBERT HALE · LONDON

ISBN 978-0-7198-1429-7

Robert Hale Limited
Clerkenwell House
Clerkenwell Green
London EC1R 0HT

www.halebooks.com

Typeset by
Derek Doyle & Associates, Shaw Heath
Printed and bound in Great Britain by
CPI Antony Rowe, Chippenham and Eastbourne

CHAPTER 1

Monday morning, and Will Grafton was where he was to be found every working day of the week, which is to say back of the counter in his grocery store. Grafton was like a fixed star in the firmament and you knew that Monday to Saturday, you would be sure to find the balding, spare-framed, bespectacled, middle-aged man in his store on Alila's main street.

The little township of Alila was one of a straggling line of settlements strung out between San Francisco and Los Angeles. Few people came there unless they had special business in the town, although since the Southern Pacific Railroad line had been built through the place, it had become somewhat more lively.

On this particular day the *Atlantic Flyer* was due to stop over at the station and Grafton's wife had taken their eldest son to watch the mighty locomotive haul the train up the slope from Tulare and into the town.

Twelve years ago Will Grafton, who was at that time a forty-year-old bachelor, had astonished everybody in town by marrying a girl half his age. It was the first and last time that this rather nondescript shopkeeper and elder of the Presbyterian church did anything liable to provoke the least remark from his neighbours. Against all expectations, the marriage had proved a glorious success and Grafton's beautiful young wife had given him three children. If ever there was a man on this Earth who was truly contented with his lot in life, it was Alila's grocer.

Although not in the slightest degree interested in railroad trains herself, Carrie Grafton enjoyed visiting the depot with her eleven-year-old son. Billy-Joe had a seemingly inexhaustible fund of knowledge about every aspect of locomotives, carriages, tracks, signals and everything else connected with trains, and it was pleasant to listen to his enthusiastic chatter.

She really didn't know where he picked up all this information, and sometimes wished that he would put as much effort into learning about the arithmetic and history he was taught at school, as he did in memorizing the wheel configurations of the various classes of locomotives which passed through the town.

'Look Mama, here it comes now,' the boy cried, as the puffing locomotive hauled into the station. 'Ain't it a grand sight?'

'Isn't, darling,' said his mother. 'Ain't is vulgar, you know.'

'Can we go closer? I'd sure like to see the driver and fireman when they get down from the cab.'

'Are they going to get out here?'

'Of course,' said the boy, scornful of his mother's abysmal ignorance in matters relating to the railroad.

'Why, they have to take on water. Please can we get closer?'

Mrs Grafton smiled down at the eager boy. 'I don't see why not.' she said.

Neither she nor her son noticed the half-dozen men who were standing on the platform as the locomotive shuddered to a halt. There was nothing remarkable about their appearance and it wasn't until they pulled their neckerchiefs up over their noses to cover half their faces, that there was anything to distinguish them from any of the other loafers hanging round the depot that morning.

Nobody knows why some children turn bad. Take George Vallence for instance: as sober, upright, respectable and God-fearing a man as was to be found anywhere in the state of Kansas. His first two sons had turned out just fine. The eldest, James, was a sheriff and his brother Peter a prosperous and well-to-do farmer.

The three younger boys, though, had never been anything but trouble to their father. They progressed in easy stages from playing hooky from school in order to poach fish, to stealing from neighbours and raising Cain in all manner of ways, until the three of them decided to move away from the district entirely.

Some said that the three young men took this step to spare their poor father the shame of having such a set of rogues blackening his family name in the town where he lived. Others though, said that Clay County was getting a little warm for the boys and that if they hung around much longer they were going on the right way to get themselves lynched. Whether or no, in the winter of 1889 Tom, Bob and Pat Vallence lit out of Kansas and headed West.

Over the course of several months, the Vallence brothers worked their way through Colorado, Utah and Nevada, raiding lonely farmhouses, holding up stages, robbing a gaming house and even stealing from lone travellers.

In the fullness of time they arrived in California, where they heard of the vast amounts of money supposedly being carried in the express cars of the railroad trains running along the Southern Pacific line. They picked up with one or two like-minded men and then laid plans for ambushing one of these trains as it stopped at a little town up in the hills called Alila.

The day the Vallences and their friends chose for this enterprise was Monday, 7 April 1890 and it was one of those glorious spring days when the sky is a deep, cerulean blue and completely cloudless. The aim was for two of the gang to hold the driver and fireman at gunpoint, to stop the train leaving the station until the robbery had been successfully accomplished, while the other four seized the express car and forced the guard to open the safe that it contained.

Billy-Joe was the first person at the station to notice that the men hanging round the locomotive had all pulled scarves or bandannas round their faces. He did not at first appreciate the significance of this, which was odd, because he had read any number of dime novels, acquired secretly from other boys at school, where behaviour of that sort was the invariable prelude to robbery and murder. Seeing it in real life in the prosaic surroundings of the local railroad station did not seem to bear any relation to the lurid line drawings of hold-ups on the covers of the trashy story books to which he and his friends were addicted.

He merely remarked to his mother casually, 'Why d'you think those fellows are covering up their faces like that? Is it 'cause they don't like the smoke and steam?'

Caroline Grafton grasped the situation almost immediately and grabbed her son's hand, meaning to hustle him away as fast as she could. She was stopped in her tracks when one of the group of men drew a pistol and announced to all those on the platform:

'Don't nobody think o' leavin', leastways, not 'til we give you leave to go.' It was clear that the men didn't want anybody rushing off to raise the alarm.

Billy-Joe's mother pulled him to her and held him tight, which proceeding caused the boy to try and wriggle free, protesting,

'Mama, don't cuddle me like that, some of the fellows from school might see me. I'll look a right baby.'

'Hush now,' said his mother, keeping him enfolded in her arms. 'You stay right where you are. These men are robbers.'

'They are?' cried the boy in excitement. 'Hey, I never saw a robber before. Wait 'til I tell the boys at school.'

The driver and fireman showed no inclination towards bravery or defiance, throwing up their hands as soon as they were bidden to do so. While one of the bandits covered them, another watched the people on the platform. They too were all intent upon doing just exactly what they were told. So far, everything was proceeding smoothly for the gang.

It was when the four other masked men went along to the express car, back of the train, that the trouble started, because as soon as the guard sitting in the barred compartment of the car that contained the safe saw them, he began shooting. As the Vallences later observed to each other, it was perfectly stupid; it wasn't, after all, *his* money that he was protecting so fiercely.

The guard exchanged shots with the four men who hoped to steal the contents of the safe and when the fireman, up by the locomotive, heard the sound of gunfire he made a bolt for it; whereupon one of the two men on the platform fired twice at him. Neither bullet hit the fleeing man, but the second, although missing its intended target, found a lodging place instead in the breast of Billy-Joe's mother, who slumped to the ground.

There was pandemonium in the station, with women screaming and various other signs of disorder. The six robbers, who had not counted on any opposition, decided to give up their attempt as a bad job and leave empty-handed. They did so in a thunder of hoofbeats.

Billy-Joe Grafton, who was quite unharmed, did not

at first appear to realize what had taken place. He knelt down and began shaking his mother urgently, trying to rouse her from what he took to be a fainting fit. It wasn't until he saw the neat little hole in the front of her dress, surrounded by a slowly spreading crimson stain, that he knew she was dead. He started wailing in despair over the lifeless body of his mother: an unearthly, high, keening sound, imbued with absolute misery, which none of those present that day ever forgot, as long as they lived.

It didn't take long for news of the tragedy to reach Will Grafton. His wife was a popular figure in the town. She taught Sunday School, went visiting the sick and always had time to listen to other folk's troubles. Most of those on the platform knew her by sight. The first that Grafton knew of it was when two members of his church walked into the store. Their faces were sombre.

'Well, friends,' said Grafton, 'what can I do for you today?'

'Will,' said one of the men, 'There's been some shooting up at the depot. A robbery went wrong.'

'A robbery?' exclaimed Grafton, horrified. 'In our town? Lord, I don't know what things are coming to.' Then he suddenly remembered that Carrie and Billy-Joe were to have been up that way. 'My, I hope my boy's all right,' he said. The look on the faces of his friends filled him with alarm.

'Billy-Joe's fine. My wife's tending to him this minute. He's not hurt.'

'Your wife's tending to him?' said Grafton, bewildered. 'I don't rightly understand. Why isn't his mother with him?'

'We're so sorry, Will,' began one of the men and in that instant, everything was revealed to the grocer and he knew without a shadow of a doubt that his wife was dead. There was a strange humming in his ears, his mouth went dry and then his legs gave way. For the first time in the whole course of his life, Will Grafton fainted.

The funeral of Caroline Grafton took place eight days later in the little burying ground behind the Presbyterian church. Before that event though, came several sensational developments. The first of these was the capture of one of the robbers, whose horse broke a leg after setting foot in a hole, as he and his partners were fleeing Alila. An angry crowd seized the man and began roughing him up, the murder of a woman being regarded with the utmost loathing and detestation. It might have gone badly for the fellow had Sheriff Jackson not arrived on the scene and taken him into custody. Even so, there were murmurs about the desirability of executing summary justice upon this wretch and the sheriff, not wanting to see a lynching in the town, made arrangements to send his prisoner to the Kern County jail at Bakersfield, to await trial.

The 11 April 1890 edition of the *Bakersfield Recorder, incorporating the Kern County Advertiser* told the story of what happened next.

Amazing Escape of Suspected Killer

Those readers who, like us, were shocked and dismayed to hear of the brutal murder of Mrs Caroline Grafton in the course of a bungled robbery at the Alila railroad depot, will be astounded at the latest developments in the case; developments which do not redound to the credit of our law-enforcement agencies. It will be recalled that the captured man had on him letters and papers which identified him as one Thomas Vallence from Kansas. The telegraph wires between Kansas and our own fair state were fairly humming in no time at all and the intelligence was soon received that this man was one of a gang, consisting chiefly of he himself and his two brothers: namely Robert and Patrick Vallence. They are well known in their own neck of the woods as scallywags and rascals of the first water and it apparently surprises nobody in Clay County, from where they hail, to learn that they have now progressed to murder.

Following the sanguinary events in Alila, the sheriff of that town, Michael Jackson, thought it prudent to have his prisoner transported to the jail at Bakersfield until he was brought to trial. The fear was that some outraged local citizenry were planning to hold an impromptu 'Necktie Party', to which the afore mentioned Thomas Vallence would be invited.

Two young deputies, whose names we have

13

been unable to ascertain, were assigned the job of escorting Vallence to Bakersfield. How shall we tell readers of the behaviour of these young men? One handcuffed himself to the suspected bandit and promptly fell asleep, the other engaged in such lively conversations with other passengers that he did not notice what his prisoner was about. It is believed that while one guard was enjoying his refreshing slumbers and the other behaving as though he were propping up the bar in a saloon, Vallence took the opportunity to abstract the key to the handcuffs from the pocket of his sleeping guardian and free himself from their restraint. When the train passed over the trestle-bridge which spans the Oshago river, the prisoner leaped through the window of the carriage into the water below. A later search failed to reveal any sign of the escaped man. We are reliably informed that the town of Alila is now seeking to engage two new deputies.

Will Grafton listened with only half his attention to the familiar words of the burial service as they were intoned at the graveside. *I am the resurrection and the life. . . . Man that is born of woman has but a short time to live. . . .* Odd how he had always found these same words so comforting and consoling when spoken at funerals he had previously attended. Maybe, he thought bitterly, that's because none of those people I saw buried before really mattered all that much to me.

There was a very large turnout for Carrie's funeral;

the whole town seemed to be there. She had surely been a popular woman. Grafton looked down at his three children, who were standing at his side. Their faces were pale and pinched; the reality of their mother's death was perhaps only now becoming plain to them as, one after another, the mourners filed past and cast clods of earth on to the coffin as it lay at the bottom of the freshly dug grave.

When he had shaken everybody's hand and accepted their whispered condolences, Grafton asked his sister if she would take the children home and sit with them for a little, while he conducted some business in town. When they were gone he directed his steps towards Sheriff Jackson's office.

In the first few days following his wife's death, Will Grafton had considered all manner of wild schemes, which chiefly centred around getting hold of the men who had murdered his wife and subjecting them to the most vicious and ingenious tortures imaginable. Then he had turned to scripture for advice. Almost the first verse which leapt out at him when he reached down his Bible was that from chapter twelve of Romans: *Vengeance is mine; I will repay, saith the Lord.*

This was so wholly to the point that he read the entire passage: *Dearly beloved, avenge not yourselves, but rather give place unto wrath: for it is written, Vengeance is mine; I will repay, saith the Lord.*

Well, thought Grafton, I reckon that just about sums up the case neatly. The Lord doesn't want me to go chasing off after those villains and shooting them or anything of that sort. Still and all, it can't be right that they should get clean away after such a crime. They must be brought to justice and I don't see why I shouldn't lend a hand there.

After he heard about Tom Vallence's escape Grafton was all the more convinced that he should involve himself in the matter, not as a private individual, but in an official capacity.

Sheriff Jackson was feeling like something of a failure on the day of Carrie Grafton's funeral. He had attended the funeral, of course, but felt that all those present were staring at him reproachfully for letting the one man to have been caught escape scot free. He got back to his office just five minutes before Will Grafton knocked hesitantly on the street door.

'Come in, Mr Grafton,' said the sheriff, feeling an excruciating sense of embarrassment at having to meet face to face with the man he had let down so badly. 'What can I do for you? Take a seat.'

'Thank you,' said Grafton, and sat down opposite Sheriff Jackson. There was an uncomfortable silence and then Grafton said: 'Sheriff, I'm not one for a lot of fancy words and chasing round the woodpile, so I'll just come straight out with it. I want you to swear me in as a deputy, issue warrants for the men who tried to hold up the *Atlantic Flyer* and then allow me to go and bring them in.'

This was so unexpected that Jackson was quite lost for words. After a space, he said, 'You, Mr Grafton? But surely you want to be with your children at a time like this? Then there's your store. . . .'

What he really meant to say, of course, was that Will Grafton was the wrong side of fifty, a finicky and precise little man who wore eyeglasses and was a grocer to boot, and that the idea of such a man hunting down and apprehending a band of train robbers was too ridiculous for words. Jackson hoped that none of this showed in his face.

'My sister will take care of the children and I have somebody who will run the store in my absence. Are there any other reasons why you shouldn't deputize me?'

'Mr Grafton, it isn't to be thought of. For one thing, you're not a young man—' began Sheriff Jackson, only for Grafton to cut in impatiently, saying:

'That's nothing to the purpose. I mind those two fellows as was escorting Vallence was half my age, but even the two of them together couldn't keep a hold of him. I couldn't do any worse than them.'

This was undeniably true and Jackson felt himself redden to hear the case set out so bluntly. He tried another tack.

'Then again, you ain't had much experience in such matters. When all's said and done, you're a grocer, not a lawman.'

'I wasn't always a grocer. Only since coming to this town. I was four years in the Provost Marshal's service during the war. I reckon I know enough about the business of being a peace officer.'

'You were in the Provost Guard? I didn't know that. Still, we must be talking twenty-five years ago. Things change.'

17

'I sure hate to push myself forward, Sheriff Jackson, but when all's said and done, what do you stand to lose? It'll only cost you my travelling expenses and if I get myself killed, then it's not your fault.'

Jackson thought the matter over for a minute or two. He could see that the man in front of him was determined to go after the men who had killed his wife and he, Mike Jackson, didn't blame him one little bit. As Grafton said, what did he stand to lose?

Jackson needed two new deputies and the first duty of any new men would be to chase after the Vallences anyway.

He said, 'You know that, if I were to swear you in, your powers would be very thin outside this county?'

'I know about jurisdictions, if that's what you mean. Give me warrants for the men and let me deal with the legal disputes.'

'What rank were you, during the war?'

'Ended as provost marshal.'

'Suppose I tell you that I won't do it?'

Will Grafton smiled bleakly. 'I can't see what would stop you, Sheriff. To speak straight, you're almost as keen as I am to see those men brought back to stand trial in California. I lost my wife, but you stand to lose your reputation. Livelihood too, I dare say. Can't see you getting voted in again next year, if you don't catch that fellow as your deputies lost.'

The sheriff opened a drawer and rummaged around in it. At length he found what he was looking for and pulled out a crumpled sheet of paper, with some printed words on it. He said to the grocer.

'Well, like you say, I got nothing to lose and maybe something to gain. Read out these here words.'

Grafton picked up the sheet and said in a loud, clear voice:

'I, William Grafton, do swear that I will faithfully execute all writs, precepts and processes directed to me as deputy sheriff of the county, or which are directed to all sheriffs of this state, or to any other sheriff especially. I can lawfully execute and true returns make, and in all things well and truly, without malice or partiality, perform the duties of deputy sheriff during my continuance therein and take only my lawful fees.

'I further swear that I will uphold the constitution of the United States and of this state, so help me God.'

'Sign it at the bottom and then date it,' said Sheriff Jackson. 'Then give it here for me to sign.' Having done this, he announced, 'Well, Mr Grafton, you are now a lawfully appointed deputy sheriff. Come by in the morning and I'll have warrants for all three of the Vallence brothers.'

The grocer thanked Jackson and stood up to leave.

'You're forgetting something, Mr Grafton,' said Sheriff Jackson. He reached again into the drawer and took something out, which he laid on the desk. It was a metal star. 'You sure about this?' he asked.

Will Grafton leaned over and picked up the star, saying, 'I never been surer of anything in my life.'

CHAPTER 2

At about the same time that Will Grafton was being sworn in as a deputy sheriff the three Vallence brothers were seated on their horses, on the outskirts of a little town in Arizona. Their aim now was to take the railroad east, in the general direction of Oklahoma.

Since fishing Tom out of the Oshago, they had made good time and also had some pretty fine luck in coming across a man carrying a substantial quantity of cash. They had no idea who this fellow was, nor how come he came to be in possession of over $700, but it meant that they would not now be obliged to ride all the hundreds of miles to Oklahoma, but could instead travel in style.

'You sure 'bout this?' asked Pat. 'Seems to me like we was doin' well enough in California.'

'You got shit for brains, or what?' enquired Tom Vallence, who happened to be the eldest of the three, 'It ain't only my neck as'll get stretched if we get found anywhere in that state again.'

'Still and all, though,' said Pat, not at all abashed, 'we wasn't doing at all badly there.'

'Why don't we hear now what Tom will tell us?' said Bob, the third of the trio. 'Seems to me that he has some kind of plan in mind.'

The three men whom the Vallences had picked up and who had helped undertake the assault on the *Atlantic Flyer*, had all decided that life with the Vallences was just that little bit too lively. Realising that they would all hang if caught after the incident at Alila, they had chosen to go their own separate ways.

'First off is where we'll need to find a few new men,' said Tom. 'Then we hit another train.'

'God almighty, Tom,' exclaimed Patrick Vallence, 'Are you out o' your mind? I reckon we had enough of those capers.'

'Shut up and listen,' said his brother, roughly, 'We learn from our mistakes is all. Takin' that train was a right smart move, we just chose the wrong location.'

'Go on,' said Bob. 'Sounds like you give the matter some little thought.'

'You're damn right I thought about it. How it all went wrong at Alila was where we was surrounded by people. Havin' to keep a heap of folk in that depot and then, when we dug up, there was a crowd just waiting to grab me when my horse went down. That won't happen where we're goin' next.'

'Go on then,' said Pat. 'Where's that?'

'Place with hardly any towns, just a bunch of settlers who ain't been there above a twelvemonth. Wherever you stop a train there, there's nobody much round to take note of it. What they used to call the Indian Nations.'

Bob Vallence rubbed his chin thoughtfully, saying, 'There may be somewhat in that. I mind last year it was opened up to settlers. They fired a starting gun and thousands of folk just stampeded in there. What's the name o' that line as runs north to south through there?'

'The Katy. Or, in full, the Missouri, Kansas and Texas Railroad. They call it the Katy, on account of the two letters for Kansas and Texas, the 'K' 'T'. It runs through places where hardly a soul lives,' said Tom. 'This here train we're getting now will take us to Oklahoma and we can work our way into the new territories from there.'

After leaving the sheriff's office Will Grafton walked slowly down main street, heading towards his house. His sister would be taking good care of the little ones and there was no hurry to get back. It might be a good time to see about arming himself.

In his attic was an old trunk containing, among other old souvenirs, the pistol which he had carried during the War between the States: an 1860 Army Colt. He doubted whether it would be wise going after a group of deadly gunmen sporting an antique like that.

He accordingly crossed the street and went into one of the few stores in town that he had never had occasion to visit. He knew Harry Springer, who owned the gunsmith's, socially, but had not before felt the need to purchase a firearm. He had finished with all that a quarter of a century earlier, following the surrender at Appomattox.

Springer greeted him affably. 'Afternoon, Mr Grafton. Hope you don't think me lacking in respect for your poor wife by opening today?'

Grafton shrugged. 'A body has to live. Didn't our Lord say, "Let the dead bury their dead"?'

Scripture was not by way of being Harry Springer's strong suit, so he limited himself to saying, 'It may be so, Mr Grafton, it may be so. Anyways, how can I help you?'

'I'd like to buy a pistol, please.'

The storekeeper shot him an odd look. 'Going hunting, are you?'

'Not precisely. I used to carry one of those old cap-and-ball pistols, but I know things have changed now.'

'That they have. You don't see such articles these days, not outside of a museum at any rate.'

'I really want something up to date, but not as heavy as these forty-fives I see everywhere. You got something in a lighter calibre than that, maybe thirty-six or thirty-eight?'

'I got a few Smith and Wessons in that calibre, which is to say, they're thirty-eights. Maybe that's what you're looking for?'

The pistol that Springer handed him felt just right in Will Grafton's hand. It had been over two decades since last he had handled a deadly weapon, but he had no doubt of his ability to manage one again. The storekeeper was eyeing him strangely as Grafton swung open the cylinder and checked that the trigger was smooth. It was odd to see the town grocer handling a pistol with such assurance.

'I want a holster for this as well, please,' said Grafton. 'Not one of those that flaps round your thigh, though. I'm looking for a shoulder holster. You know, the kind that you can keep your gun under your arm?'

'Mr Grafton, it's no affair of mine, but might I ask what all this is in aid of?'

'I'm going away for a few days and I don't want to fall prey to robbers and suchlike. It's no mystery.'

By the time he left Springer's store, the grocer had a short-barrelled thirty eight revolver tucked away out of sight under his jacket and his pockets were sagging with ammunition.

Bryan Bertram McKinley, known to his intimate friends as B.B., was in a foul mood. You might think that being chief of the detective force of the Missouri, Kansas and Texas Railroad Company would entitle you to a few perks and bonuses, but only recently his employers had furnished ample evidence that this was not at all the case.

The source of B.B. McKinley's grievance was a simple one. A week earlier he had identified and apprehended, single-handed, a dangerous individual who had staged a robbery at the depot in Junction City. More to the point, the Katy, as the company was known for short, had been offering a reward of $500 for information leading to this man's arrest.

Now McKinley was not so sanguine as to expect the whole of the reward money; he would have been quite satisfied with half. His employers, though, took the line that since he was being paid a good wage to catch thieves and other types, it was a bit rich for him to expect to get the reward money as well, when he laid hands on a wanted man.

Previously he had always been able to cut a deal over such matters, but with the cut-throat way the railroad lines were currently being operated in competition with each other, the Katy was desperate to cut their costs to the bone. He received nothing.

Three days later McKinley was still brooding about being, as he saw it, cheated out of that $500. He was seated in a window seat of a train heading south to the Oklahoma Territory. In another few minutes they would be arriving in Parsons. The company wanted him to check the line for likely spots for any ambush robberies, this being an especially popular kind of crime lately.

The fact was, B.B. McKinley was in serious financial difficulties and that reward money would have gone some way to solving his troubles. He had one son at college, two daughters still at home, and a mortgage on that home. Not to mention where he also had a heap of gambling debts and was fond of visiting prostitutes in the towns through which he passed. On top of this, McKinley was partial, too partial said some, to a drop of whiskey. He owed money left, right and centre at the moment and where the means to settle those debts was going to come from, he didn't rightly know.

While he was racking his brains for a way to get hold of a little extra cash, McKinley became aware of an altercation going on behind him. He craned his head round and saw a young man arguing with a ticket collector. The man was growing agitated and raising his voice.

'I tell you now, I got on at Chanute and that's where I'm a-paying from.'

The conductor, a white-haired old fellow with a long, droopy mustache, said,

'I'm not so sure about that, young man. Can you describe the station at Chanute or tell who sold you this ticket as you say you lost?'

McKinley stood up and walked down the carriage. He said to the old man, 'You know who I am?'

'Why, yes sir, Mr McKinley, sure I recognize you.'

'Let me handle this and I'll give you the fare when I collect it.'

The elderly conductor was only too happy to leave this unpleasant young man to the detective and went bustling off down the train. McKinley stood there for a moment and then, without any warning at all, reached down, grabbed the front of the man's coat and hauled him to his feet.

'Come on son,' he said quietly. 'Let's you and me go for a little walk.' So saying, he marched the fellow along to the end of the carriage, where there was nobody about.

The train was pulling into Parsons, which suited McKinley's purposes just fine. He said, 'Hand me your wallet.'

'You say what?' said the young man angrily. 'Why, I'll be damned—' He got no further than this, because McKinley struck him a sudden sharp blow in his stomach. The fellow folded up like a pocket rule, retching and coughing.

'Let's try that again,' said McKinley. 'Hand me your wallet.' When there was no response he began going through the young man's pockets methodically, until he unearthed a leather pocket book. A quick glance inside showed that McKinley had been right and this was going to be worth the trouble. He extracted three fifty-dollar bills, then stuck the pocket book back into the fellow's coat.

'I'm fining you a hundred dollars for disorderly behaviour and another fifty for travelling without a ticket,' he explained.

The train stopped only briefly at Parsons, there being few passengers getting on or off. As it began to pull out of the station McKinley opened the door and pitched the young man out of the train and on to the platform. It was a calculated risk, but something about the fellow told McKinley that he wouldn't be making any official complaint. At a guess, he had made the money illegally himself and would not be wishing to draw attention to his loss, for fear of inviting enquiry about where his money had come from in the first place. The chief of detectives was a good judge of such things.

As he took his seat again B.B. McKinley was feeling pretty braced with himself. Two minutes work for $150 wasn't bad going, not bad going at all!

Grafton's sister Martha was a widow, who had moved to Alila to be close to her only remaining family. She and her husband had never been blessed with children of their own. She adored her niece and two nephews and spent as much time at her brother's house as she could.

It was customary to have mourners back at the house after the funeral, but Martha had blocked the idea indignantly, on behalf of her brother. She thought that the children needed to get back to normal as soon as possible and come to terms with the tragedy which had befallen them.

When Will came through the door that afternoon his sister was grappling with an abstruse theological question. Six year-old Ella wanted to know whether her mama would be able to hear if she, Ella, whispered something to her in the course of her prayers. If so, then how come those still on Earth didn't themselves hear all that was going on in the promised land? Did the sound of voices only travel one way? Will Grafton's timely arrival rescued his sister from what promised to be a most complicated discussion.

'I'm glad you're back,' said Martha. 'I'm sure that whatever business it was could have waited 'til today was over.'

'Not really,' replied her brother apologetically. 'It was kind of urgent.'

Ella went up to her father and threw her arms around him. He picked her up, and then his sons also appeared: eleven-year-old Billy-Joe and nine-year-old Linton. They too went to their father and were also embraced by him. For a second or two Grafton stood there, letting the love of his children flow through him

28

like an electric current.

Then he said, 'Let me speak to Aunt Martha for a bit and then I'll be at your disposal. Off you go now.' Reluctantly, the three youngsters went off together.

Martha made some coffee and asked her brother, 'How are you feeling now?'

'It's hard to say. I thought the funeral would make me feel better, but it hasn't.'

'It's only a little over a week, Will. You don't heal from a wound like that in a few days.'

When the two of them were seated at the big pine table in the kithcen, Grafton said,

'Could you move in here for a week or two and take care of the children?'

'It would give me nothing but pleasure,' said Martha. 'You need time to grieve and want me to keep the children occupied. I see that.'

'That's not quite how it is, Martha. I need to go away for a spell.'

His sister looked at him in amazement. 'Go away? Wherever to?'

'I aim to find the men who killed Caroline.'

'Don't tell me that you are seeking vengeance. I never heard of aught of that sort come to any good. What do you want, to kill them as killed Caroline?'

'Lord forbid,' said Grafton piously. 'I have just been sworn in as a deputy.' He fished around in his pocket and brought out the star to show his sister. 'It's all open and above board, I am going to find those men and then bring them back here to stand trial.'

'You, Will? Have you lost your mind? You're fifty-two

years of age, I never heard of such a thing.'

'We both know that being in the grocery trade isn't all I've done in my life. I tracked men down before and brought them to justice. You think I would have been appointed provost marshal if I didn't know about bringing in suspects and such?'

'William Grafton,' said Martha, and the fact that she used his full name told her brother that she was in great earnest, 'That was twenty-four years ago, if it was a day. You have changed a good deal since those days.'

'Happen so, but I mind I'll have no peace on this Earth if I don't set out to do what I may. I will not rest easy in my bed while I know that the men who shot my wife are roaming free. I have thought long on this and prayed hard. I will do it.'

'Well, when you say you'll do a thing I know you'll do it. I see I can't talk you out of it. Of course I'll stay here and tend to those little ones. You know I will.'

So it was that the next day Will Grafton handed over the running of his shop to a smart young fellow who had been asking him for a job, collected three warrants from Sheriff Jackson and set off in search of the men who had murdered his beloved wife.

CHAPTER 3

A week after Caroline Grafton's funeral the Vallence brothers were preparing for their next train robbery, which they intended to carry out in the Oklahoma Territory.

Until 1889 the five civilized Indian tribes had occupied this land, which had been granted to them in perpetuity by solemn and binding covenants signed by the government in Washington. The land had been known as the Indian Nations and was closed to white settlers.

The time came, though, when more land was needed for homesteading and so the Indians had to surrender their sovereignty and become part of Oklahoma. Although the area was now theoretically subject to the laws of Oklahoma, it was still a wild sort of place where you were unlikely to encounter any lawmen. A perfect hunting ground, in fact, for men like the Vallence brothers.

It had not taken the three Vallences too long to find four new members for their gang. The former Indian

Nations was full of drifters, fugitives, outlaws and men on the lookout to make a quick buck. Three of the new recruits were white men and their names were Joe Short, Charlie Byrne and Fenton Sadler. There was also a half-breed Choctaw who called himself Wolfrider. None of them ever found out if he had a proper name as well.

The first train that was targeted was simply designated Passenger Train No. 2 by the Katy and it was scheduled to run through the territory from Denniston in Texas, all the way up to Parsons in Kansas. The gang proposed to ambush it near a place called Muskogee. Not actually in the town; they had already seen the evils that attended such a course of action when they carried out the abortive raid at Alila. No, this time, they would take it about five miles south of the town, where there wouldn't be anybody to interfere. There was a little way halt, where passengers could signal for the train to stop.

Tom Vallence figured that seven riders could look a mite suspicious, hanging round, and that the train driver might just take it into his head to keep going rather than meekly stop for them. He hit upon a right cunning plan to avoid alarming anybody and it was this. Near to the place where passengers could wait there was a wooden shed full of various supplies that trains might need: things such as cans of lamp oil, a few sacks of coal and so on. They bust open the door to this building and there was just about room in there for seven horses, if they were all squashed together. Six of the gang also squeezed in as Passenger Train No.2

hove into sight, leaving Pat Vallence alone to signal that he wished to board the train.

Pat looked about the most respectable of the brothers and he had made a point of shaving the day before. There was nothing about his appearance to awaken any apprehensions in the driver or fireman, so the train was brought to a halt. Whereupon Pat Vallence leaped into the cab and pulled his pistol, desiring the driver and fireman both to step down. At the same moment six heavily armed men emerged from the wooden shed, leading their horses with them.

Having ensured that the train could not proceed, Pat said to the fireman,

'You show my friends here to the express car and help them gain access. Otherwise we goin' to kill you.'

It was tolerably clear to the passengers looking out of the windows that this was a hold-up. The more seasoned travellers began hiding their valuables and money beneath seats. Some train robbers went through the length of the train, stealing the personal belongings of passengers, especially those who looked prosperous. The Vallences and their accomplices had little interest in taking men's watches and women's gold earbobs, though. They were aiming a little higher.

The fireman walked to the back of the train with three of the gang, then climbed up the steps and rapped on the door of the last but one carriage.

'It's me, Dave,' he said. 'Will you let me in?'

The men standing around the door heard somebody say from within,

'Hell, you know I can't do that. I ain't 'llowed to

open this door anywhere other than at those stations on the list.'

'You don't open that door right now, we goin' to shoot your friend Dave here,' announced Tom Vallence. 'And then when we done that, we goin' to dynamite this here carriage and get in that way. You live or you die, friend, but either way, we're a-coming in.'

There was a pause, which was followed by the click of a lock being turned. The bluff had worked; the Vallences had no dynamite and had the express messenger in the car refused to open up there was little they could have done.

Inside the windowless carriage was a barred compartment at the end of which was a large safe. Clinton Jeffries, the express messenger, had a key to open the gate that allowed access to the safe; what he didn't have, though, was the combination to open the safe.

He told the bandits this, but of course they assumed he was lying. He was dragged over to the safe, a gun put to his head and he was informed that either he opened the safe or he would be dead within the minute. There then followed one of those extraordinary incidents which demonstrate the truth of the old adage: that life is stranger than fiction.

The 25 April 1890, edition of the *Stillwater Gazette* carried an account of what happened next, sent to them by their correspondent in Parsons, Kansas;

When the train reached here Express Messenger Jeffries had not fully recovered from his experiences, and in a talk with your reporter stated that

34

he did not know how he had opened the safe, as he was ignorant of the combination, and that if he had to do it over again, he could not do so to save his life! Nevertheless, with the encouragement of a six-shooter hovering a fraction of an inch from his ear, Jeffries somehow succeeded in gaining access to the stout iron box's interior. He was then faced with the unenviable task of revealing to the desperadoes that the safe was quite innocent of cash.

'The hell d'you mean,' growled Tom Vallence, 'There's no money?' He grabbed a handful of the elaborately printed documents that lay inside the safe and eyed them uncomprehendingly. 'What is this shit?'

'They're bonds. Bonds and stocks.' Jeffries was trembling so badly that he could hardly get the words out. 'For banks, you know.'

'You ain't got any money at all?'

'There's only what you see here.'

So it was that for the second time the Vallence brothers held up a train and gained not a single cent from doing so. They vented their frustration, before galloping off, by shooting up the train from outside, smashing the windows and causing injuries to a couple of passengers from flying fragments of broken glass.

The four new associates of the Vallences were a little disconcerted at this failure and wondered if they had hitched up with the wrong men. Fortunately, the next robbery was to be a great success, which restored their faith in their new partners.

B.B. McKinley was mightly put out when he heard about the hold-up of Passenger Train No. 2 at Muskogee. He had passed through that way less than a week earlier and now some scoundrel had staged a raid there. His bosses in the railroad company were not best pleased by the event either and McKinley was earnestly entreated to liven his ideas up and start providing some security, which is what they were paying him to do.

McKinley was angered by this, but it sowed the seed in his mind of an audacious scheme that might solve all his money worries at one swoop and give him a little left over into the bargain.

The day after he had received a dressing-down from two directors of the Missouri, Kansas and Texas Railroad Company, McKinley wired his cousin, whom he had not seen for some while, asking him to contact him urgently in connection with a matter which would be greatly to his advantage. He also resolved privately that he would not over-exert himself in trying to prevent another robbery on the Katy; at least not until his cousin turned up.

Will Grafton was staying in a little hotel in Parsons, an establishment much patronized by commercial travellers and salesmen. He was there when the train hit by the Vallences pulled into town. Even without the excited speculations which he soon heard in the streets of Parsons, he knew at once that the men he was seeking had been behind this latest attack.

There would have been no purpose in acquiring a horse before he left Alila because, even when he was in the army, Grafton had been a hopeless rider. Fortunately, his duties in the Provost Guard had not required much facility in that direction and he knew that at this late stage of his life there was little point in starting to remedy the shortcoming. In any case, the idea of the fifty-two-year-old grocer riding the range and pursuing a gang of outlaws on horseback was so ridiculous as to bring a smile to his lips, in spite of his grief.

It had taken three trains to bring Grafton to Parsons and he was hoping that Sheriff Jackson would not think that he had been extravagant. Although it was over twenty-five years since he had had any dealings with law enforcement, Will Grafton still had a brain in his head and it had not taken too much calculating to see where the Vallences would be heading. The California newspapers had exchanged notes with their fellow journalists in Kansas and had built up a pretty good portrait of the three brothers. There had even been artists' sketches in one paper.

When he was with the Provost Guard, Grafton had been called upon to track down fugitives: criminals and deserters in the main. He had been very successful at this, purely and simply by asking himself the question, *What would I do, were I that fellow?* He had used the same method when mulling over the likely course of action which the Vallences might pursue.

Clearly, they would not want to stay in California,

when public feeling was running so high against them and they were wanted for murder. The sea lay to the west and the quickest way to leave the state would be to ride east. Grafton had got down his children's atlas and looked where that might lead.

The men wouldn't want to return to Kansas, where there were apparently a number of outstanding matters, chiefly involving the stealing of horses and the beating near to death of a man in a bar-room brawl. But right next to Kansas, to the south, were the Indian Territories, which were by all accounts still full of fugitives and outlaws. That was where they'd be heading, for a bet. And once there, what else would they do but try to hold up another train? They hadn't had a whole lot of luck with their last enterprise in this field, but Grafton knew what habitual criminals were like. They would try again.

The mood in Red Rock Canyon, where the Vallences and their followers were camped out, was not cheerful. It was two days since the abortive robbery of Passenger Train No. 2 and it took no great ability to foretell the future to realize that unless they laid hands on some money soon, the other four men in the group would be drifting away and joining up with some more profitable outfit: maybe somebody who actually knew how to arrange a hold-up which netted some return.

Sensing the mood of the men, even his brother Pat was becoming a little fresh with him and hinting that Tom might not be the best member of the Vallence family to lead them, Tom Vallence announced on the evening of 23 April, that the next day they were going to take the Katy *Flyer* as it passed near to their hideout.

Wolfrider, the Choctaw, was unwise enough to ask, 'Are we like to get any money from this raid, or will we just be smashing a few windows?'

The brothers were well familiar with Tom Vallence's temper, but it took the young half-breed by surprise, because the words were no sooner out of his mouth than Tom Vallence had jumped up and knocked him sprawling in the dirt. He followed this by pulling out the Bowie knife that he kept in a sheath at his belt and pressing the blade of this hard against the man's neck.

'You speak so to me again,' he said in a quiet, conversational tone of voice, 'an' before God, I'm a-goin' to cut your damn throat.'

'Hey, I didn't mean nothing by it,' said Wolfrider, 'I was only joshing.'

'Joshin', was you?' said Tom. 'Let me hear you doin' of it again and I'll kill you.'

This was all plain enough and nobody else seemed inclined to make jokes about the projected robbery. Trying to smooth things over a little and lower the temperature, Bob Vallence said,

'Tell us what you got in mind.'

Tom got off the young Choctaw and replaced his knife in its sheath. He said,

'I know for certain sure that the Katy *Flyer* is carrying two thousand dollars in gold tomorrow night, taking it up to Junction City.'

Nobody felt like asking Tom Vallence the source of his information and they never did learn how he came to find out about this shipment of bullion.

He continued, 'While you boys was scratching your arses yesterday and playing with yourselves while we waited for that train, I took the trouble to steal something useful from that shed we broke into.'

He reached into the leather saddle-bag at his side and withdrew a bull's-eye oil lamp. 'This here's a warning lantern. You'll note as the lens is red, for danger. Those men working on the railroad use such things to warn trains of some hazard up ahead, tellin' 'em to stop.'

'You say we can use that there to stop the train in the dark?' asked Charlie Byrne. 'That is one smart idea.'

'Ain't it, though?' said Tom Vallence, by no means impervious to flattery of this sort. 'What's more, it's a-goin' to work, too.'

On the evening that the Vallence brothers hit the Katy *Flyer*, Will Grafton was sitting in his hotel room, writing a letter to his children. This is what he wrote:

24/4/90

Dear Billy-Joe, Linton and Ella,
I have been thinking a lot about all three of you today. When you are a little older, you might understand why I had to go off like this and leave you, just at the very time you want me to stay close to you.

You all know that some bad men were responsible for the loss of your mama, may she rest peacefully. Well, Sheriff Jackson, who is a good man, engaged me to come and look for the men who hurt your mama and bring them back to Alila, so that they can be taken to court. Only think on that; your pa working for the sheriff, instead of weighing out biscuits in his shop!

Sometimes, children, grown-up persons have to do some mighty disagreeable things, even when they don't want to do them at all. (Like when it's time to go to bed for you three and you don't want to go upstairs in the least degree, but you still have to do it!) It's something like that that I am doing now.

I want to be at home with the three of you, but it's my duty to be out here, looking for the men who did that terrible thing to your mama. Maybe your Aunt Martha will be able to explain this better than I am can. I hope you are all being good for your Aunt and recollect that I love you all very much. Remember me in your prayers, as I remember you in mine every night.

With much love from your Pa.

Tom Vallence's information, wherever he had got it from, was proving to be spot on. Six riders waited to one side in the pitch dark and sure enough, they saw the lights of the train bearing down upon them. Tom had lit the red lantern earlier and he stood in the middle of the track, swinging it from side to side. It would be impossible for the men in the cab of the locomotive not to see it.

They heard the squealing of the brakes being applied when the Katy *Flyer* was still some good half mile away. It took a little time to bring such a mighty beast to a halt. Although he had been ready to jump to one side if the train didn't manage to stop in time, in actual fact Tom didn't need to. The locomotive ground to a halt twenty feet in front of him. The driver leaned out of his cab and called into the darkness,

'What's to do?'

Tom Vallence set the lantern carefully down and ran to the cab. He hauled himself up the steps and whipped out his pistol, saying,

'This is what's to do, it's a hold-up!'

The fireman muttered a disgusted oath and then he and the driver were ushered down on to the trackside. By this time the other men had ridden up and were dismounting.

There was no difficulty persuading the man in the express car to open up. He wasn't about to risk his life for his employer and just did as he was ordered. The gold was there all right, and it wasn't even in a safe. Just five gold bars, each weighing precisely one pound, were packed into a carpetbag being transported in the express car. It had been thought wise to carry it in this casual way for the very purpose of avoiding the attention of robbers.

Everything was going as smooth as clockwork, until somebody shot Charlie Byrne in the back as he was standing by the track.

There were on the train two men who didn't have the sense that the good Lord gave a goat. They were carrying pistols, but had little idea of how to use them. Some men were like that; they had the strange notion that having a gun at your hip made you look big and tough.

These men were travelling in the company of two young women, who had picked up with them purely because they were the sort to be impressed by boasting and braggadocio. It didn't help matters either, that the men had got themselves pretty well liquored-up during the journey, which had the natural effect of dulling whatever good sense they *did* have.

As soon as it became obvious that a hold-up was taking place the girls, who were themselves a little the worse for wear from imbibing ardent spirits, started to press the men as to what they proposed to do. They said things like:

'Lord, we thought from all you was saying that you boys were up to all these games and could settle an affair like this easy enough.'

At last one of the wretched young fellows felt that his honour was being impugned, whereupon he leaned out of the window and fired at the bandits, purely by chance hitting one of them. They were wholly unprepared for the response which this action provided, because a fusillade of shots was immediately directed at them.

The other passengers threw themselves to the floor, as did the two girls who had goaded the boy on. He was too slow, though, and three bullets took him, two of which inflicted mortal wounds. He fell back into his seat and proceeded to die.

Having got the gold, the Vallences and their men did not see any need to linger further, despite the shooting. They had it in mind that once one man commences to shoot like that, it is apt to encourage others to follow suit. Charlie Byrne wasn't dead, nor did he seem to be gravely injured. Leastways, he was able to mount his horse unaided, which was all that was needed at that point.

While all this was going on down in the Territories, Will Grafton was laying his plans just across the border in Kansas. He had ascertained that the railroad line running from Texas to Kansas was a single track, with various passing places. These were seldom used, because the trains running along the line were not all that frequent.

It appeared to Grafton that if he were just to travel backwards and forward on that line, from north to south and then back again, then he had an excellent chance of being on the spot if the Vallences should take it into their heads to knock over another train.

That was a good beginning, but he didn't especially want to spend the next week just sitting on trains. There must be a way of working out which trains were most likely to be targets for the outlaws. It must also be taken into account, of course, that the Vallence brothers weren't the only gang preying on railroads at that time, not by a long sight.

There now occurred one of those curious coincidences that strike randomly from time to time. Grafton took it into his head to ask around about which trains might be particularly attractive to robbers, and he chose to do this in one of the larger saloons in Parsons.

It had been some years since he had drunk in a saloon. Grafton had forsworn strong liquor after the war, having seen the evil effects that whiskey and ale had upon men. Still and all, saloons were certainly locations where men talked and, as well as that, their tongues were often looser than they were under usual circumstances. The biggest saloon in town appeared to be an establishment called The Lucky Horseshoe and it was accordingly towards there that Grafton directed his steps that evening.

So it was that at about the time that the gun battle erupted in and around the Katy *Flyer*, Will Grafton was standing at the bar, feeling most uncomfortable and wondering whether it would strike anybody as odd were he to ask for a glass of buttermilk.

CHAPTER 4

In the end Will Grafton lost his nerve and decided to order something more in keeping with being in a saloon. Instead of buttermilk he asked for a glass of porter. He could, he supposed, always sip it slowly, and a pint of porter would not be likely to turn him into a slobbering drunkard.

Now Grafton might have been a God-fearing and respectable man, but he was not a naïve person. He knew very well that it wouldn't do to ask about the trains running through the Territories without having a reasonable explanation for his curiosity. So it was that he turned to the portly, pleasant looking middle aged man standing next to him and said,

'Hope you don't mind me opening a conversation like this, us being strangers and all?'

'Don't mind at all,' said the man. 'You go ahead now.'

'Well, that's right neighbourly of you. It's a question concerning the trains running from here to Texas.'

'Yes?' said the other man. 'Ask away, but I mightn't

know the answer. Happen you'd be better going down to the depot in the morning.'

'Well now, I thought about that, of course,' said Grafton, 'but I'm afraid they might think my question a little odd.'

'Oh,' said the man, looking with new interest at Grafton. 'How's that?'

'It's like this. I don't come from these here parts. I'm travelling down to Texas on business and might be carrying a large sum of money with me.'

'I'm honoured by your confidence,' said the other. 'What is it you want to know?'

'Naturally, I don't want to get robbed on the way and I hear that trains passing through what used to be the Indian Nations are prone to being attacked by outlaws.'

A look of annoyance flickered across the man's face, although Grafton didn't notice it. He continued,

'Anyway, here's my question. Do you know of any trains heading south in the next day or two that might be likely to attract any such robbers? Maybe because they're carrying a lot of cash or something like that? If so, then I could just avoid a train like that and take one that is less apt to be a target.'

'Well now, it so happens that you have come to the right shop for that, so to speak,' said the stranger. 'I don't know the answer just now to your enquiry, but I've a friend who works on the Katy, that's what folk in these parts call the railroad line you want to travel on. I'll be seeing him later and then I can ask him for you. Tell me now, where are you staying?'

Grafton told him.

'I will be sure to drop by tomorrow morning with the information you are seeking. Say, who shall I ask for at the hotel?'

'My name's Grafton, Will Grafton.'

'I'm Bryan Bertram McKinley, but my friends generally call me B.B.'

After robbing the Katy *Flyer*, the Vallences plainly could not return to their old hideaway, which was barely a mile from the scene. Bob Vallence, though, had scouted out a new spot where they could hole up for a day or two. As the crow flies, it was five miles from the site of their ambush, but since the way led through a maze of little gullies and ravines, it took almost two hours to get there after the robbery.

There was no percentage in hurrying and maybe having your horse break a leg in the dark. Such things could of course happen even in broad daylight, as Tom's little misfortune in Alila had shown, but the odds were multiplied considerably when you were riding through rugged country and threading your way along dried-up watercourses.

A line of hills separated the gang from the scene of their latest attack, and the Vallences thought it would be safe enough to light a fire. After all, nobody was going to see the smoke on a night such as this. They would have to be a mite more careful when daybreak came, but for now it was worth having a fire to warm them and give them the opportunity to brew up some coffee.

It wasn't until they stopped that it became apparent how badly Byrne was hurt. He somehow managed to slither down from his horse, but he was surely in poor shape. Almost the first thing he said when he was on the ground was,

'I'm bitter cold.'

There was enough tumbleweed and sticks for them to get a cheerful blaze going in a short time and everybody was pleased at the prospect of getting some hot coffee inside them. Everybody, that was, except Charlie Byrne, who, even when the fire was going, repeated his complaint of being cold. Then he said,

'I need a doctor.'

Now the good thing, at least from the point of view of the Vallence brothers, about the four men as they had picked up with, was that none of the four had been well known to each other before they began riding with the Vallences. This meant that there was little chance of two or three of them banding together to oppose anything that the Vallences had in mind.

In the present case, this meant that none of them was likely to support Byrne in his appeals for a doctor. It was not, of course, to be thought of. A man with a bullet wound in the back fetching up in need of medical attention anywhere within a hundred miles of where they were would signal unmistakably that here was a member of the gang that had hit the Katy *Flyer*.

Tom sought to reassure the injured man, clapping him on the shoulder and saying in a hearty voice,

'Ah, what ails you man? You'll be right as a trivet by and by, just you see.'

'I'm hurt bad. Real bad. I mind the bullet's still in me. I need a sawbones to dig it out.'

'Don't say so,' said Bob cheerfully. 'You'll be fine.'

Charlie Byrne got unsteadily to his feet.

'No, it ain't true. If'n I don't get to a doctor right soon, I'm done for.' He turned to the three men who were not Vallences, saying, 'Ain't that right, you boys? You can see I need to get help?'

The other men turned pointedly away, refusing to meet Charlie Byrne's eyes.

Tom Vallence said, 'Let me tell you, once for all, nobody's leavin' here 'til I say so. So you just set back down again, Byrne. You hear what I tell you?'

For a moment it seemed as though the man might be about to defy this edict but, realizing that he had nobody to support him, he sat down and said again, 'I'm cold.'

When McKinley left the Lucky Horseshoe, he felt most satisfied with the way that things were shaping up. He had long had a private theory that people were gathering information about the trains running through the Territories and then passing it on to those who actually carried out the robberies. Unless he was very much mistaken, he had just spent the last few minutes talking to one of these spies and informers. That fellow sipping cautiously at his glass of ale was just too good to be true. The man was playing some deep game of his own or his name wasn't B.B. McKinley. Wanting to travel by a safe train indeed; he'd never heard the like!

It was therefore with a sense of enormous satisfaction that McKinley headed down to the telegraph office to see if there were any messages waiting for him. There were two. One was from his immediate superior, asking for a report, and the other was from his cousin Jacob, who sent word that he would be arriving in Parsons sometime in the next two days.

McKinley decided to take a turn round the streets, smoking a cigar and working out what next he should do. Jacob was a fine fellow for an operation of this sort. The man had no nerves to speak of and was even harder and more merciless than McKinley himself, which was really saying something. He needed to be in his line of work, of course. You wouldn't want to be sensitive and compassionate, doing the sort of things that cousin Jacob did.

What he needed now was for those Vallences to carry out another robbery somewhere on the Katy. If only that could happen before Jacob arrived, then he reckoned that the two of them should have it made.

In his little hotel room, Will Grafton knelt by the side of the bed, saying his prayers. Tonight, he kept them fairly brief and to the point.

'Oh Lord, please look after my children in my absence. Take a care too of my sister Martha. I hope that I am doing your will and not undertaking this present task in a spirit of vaingloriousness. Please guide me in your paths. I ask this in your son's name. Amen.'

When he had said his prayers, Grafton reviewed the

day's events and was, on the whole, pleased with how it was going. One thing that had been troubling him slightly was his decision not to wear the star that Sheriff Jackson had given him. He wondered if that meant that he was in effect engaging in a deception. Were sheriffs and their deputies obliged to identify themselves openly at all times?

After turning the matter over in his mind he decided that he would put the star on when he boarded the train heading south to Texas.

So tender had Will Grafton's conscience become since leaving the army a quarter-century ago that he was also worried about the concealed weapon which he was carrying. Was it fair to go round like this, appearing to be unarmed? Should he not declare to all comers that he could, if need be, resort to deadly force? In the end, he decided that he would need to seek guidance from scripture and prayer about that one.

As he climbed into bed the memory of Carrie struck Grafton with devastating force. He recalled getting into bed with her at night, turning out the lamp and then holding each other. He felt the lack of her like he had had an arm or leg amputated. It was a loss that he knew would never be fully healed, but finding the men responsible would go some little way towards making things right. He turned out the lamp and then whispered into the darkness, 'I'm doing it for you, Carrie.'

Charlie Byrne died hard. For all that they had chaffed him along and said he'd be all right, all three of the

Vallences knew that he was mortally wounded. The three others probably guessed as much too. About an hour after they had all wrapped themselves up in their blankets to sleep, Byrne began groaning. At least, it started with groaning and then this turned into moans and cries.

At first the others were as sympathetic as they could be, in a rough and ready kind of way. They said things like,

'Hey, you all right there, man?' or 'Jesus Byrne, sorry you're hurting so bad.'

After the first hour of this, though, the novelty wore off and they started wishing that if the man were going to die, he'd just get it over with as quickly and quietly as possible.

An hour later the other six men were shouting at Charlie Byrne to shut up and keep quiet. His cries were now of a feverish intensity and he knew very well that he was dying. It was not only the fact that the others wanted to sleep that caused them to be so sharp with the injured man. Byrne was a horrible instance of what could happen to any one of them in their chosen line of work. It was sheer chance that that bullet had found Charlie Byrne's back and not their own. While he was shouting and hollering like that, it was a constant reminder of their own mortality and the uncertainty that attended their way of life.

The cries of pain subsided after a space and the six men who were not on the point of death drifted uneasily back to sleep. Then Byrne began raving about God.

'Oh Lord, I ain't a-ready to come to you yet,' he shouted. 'I been a sinner. Only let me recover and I'll live a better life. I don't want to die.' This went on for half an hour, until nobody was able to sleep.

In the end it was Tom Vallence who settled the fellow down. The other men saw a shadowy figure get up and go over to where the delirious man was shouting and praying. They heard Tom Vallence's voice saying in a soothing way,

'Hey, it's all right, man. We're all here with you. The Lord ain't about to take you away yet, you'll be fine. I'm goin' to set here with you a space and then you can sleep. It'll be all right.'

This was so unlike what his brothers knew of Tom, that they immediately suspected something. The other men though, who didn't know him at all, thought that he was revealing a hitherto unsuspected and caring side of his nature.

Ten minutes later Charlie Byrne had quietened down. This was not to be wondered at, because the man squatting next to him had smothered him to death with his own blanket. After he was sure that Byrne was really dead Tom Vallence got up and went back to where he had been sleeping, and they all rested peacefully until dawn.

The news of the latest hold-up down in the Territories reached Parsons by telegraph some twelve hours after the event itself. One of the first to hear about it was the chief of detectives for the Missouri, Kansas and Texas Railroad Company, who was enjoying a late breakfast in his hotel. A boy came rushing in with an urgent telegram from his employers, telling him what had chanced and desiring him to contact them 'at his earliest convenience'.

It might have been thought that this latest news would have thrown B. B. McKinley into a state of despondency, but it had the very opposite effect upon him, for after reading the telegram, a broad smile spread across his not unintelligent face.

It is often the case that outlaws and lawmen have more in common with each other than they do with ordinary folk. You might, in a sense, say that they are both playing the same game, although of course being on opposing teams. In this case the Vallence Gang could hardly have done anything more in keeping with McKinley's wishes or more likely to advance his own prospects. He hoped that his cousin would arrive in Parsons that day, because this was very definitely a case of striking while the proverbial iron was hot.

After finishing up his breakfast in a leisurely fashion, McKinley wandered down to the telegraph office and sent a reply to his bosses. If only his cousin Jacob would move himself and get down here, then they would be in business.

Will Grafton heard about the robbery of the Katy *Flyer* as he walked round town that morning. He had expected the fellow whom he had met last night in the Golden Horseshoe to drop by the hotel, as he had promised, but there was no sign of him. He stood on the sidewalk, listening with half an ear to the conversations going on around him.

'Two thousand dollars in gold . . .'

'Those Vallence boys, for sure . . .'

'Can you believe it?'

'Those Territories need cleaning up . . .'

Then he caught the name of the man with whom he had struck up the conversation the previous night:

'That McKinley needs to get on the case . . .'

Grafton had all the well-bred and respectable man's horror of appearing to have been eavesdropping on another's conversation, but this was so important that he thought himself justified in ignoring the social conventions.

'Excuse me,' he said to the two men who had been standing near by, chatting, 'Would you two be talking of a man called McKinley? Dark-looking party, with a mustache? About forty years of age and running a little to fat?'

'Yes, B.B. McKinley. What of it?'

'You'll have to forgive me,' said Grafton meekly, 'I'm new around here. Who is this McKinley?'

The man he spoke to was tempted to tell this stranger that he was damned impertinent for interrupting a private conversation in this way, and that he could go to the devil, but he also liked to display his superior knowledge to all and sundry. So he said shortly:

'B.B. McKinley is chief of detectives for the railroad line, that is to say the Missouri, Kansas and Texas line. It's his proper business to stop robberies on the Katy and some are asking what he is doing to that end.'

'Thank you. I'm greatly obliged to you.'

'You're very welcome. Was there anything else we could help you with, or might we now continue with our conversation?'

As he walked off Grafton's mind was racing. So that man who had recommended that he ask at the depot about anything relating to trains was actually working for the railroad? Well, he'd kept that quiet and no mistake. But what possible motive could he have had for being so cagy? It was a regular conundrum.

You didn't need to be a medical doctor to see that Charlie Byrne had choked to death, rather than dying from any bullet wound in his back. His face was suffused with blood and had little broken red bruises on his cheeks; the sort of thing you see in somebody who's been hanged. There didn't seem to be any percentage in drawing attention to any of this, though, and the polite fiction was maintained that the poor fellow must have bled to death in the night.

You might have thought that after the brilliantly successful robbery that the Vallence gang had conducted not twelve hours since they would be nicely settled for a time as regards money. This was not at all the case, as soon became apparent when the six of them examined closely their booty from the previous night. True, they had acquired five pounds weight of pure, certified gold bullion.

The problem was, though, that it was in the form of ingots, each one covered with various numbers and identifying marks. Of course, pure gold being so soft, there was nothing to stop them obliterating the markings, but how the hell do you spend a pound of gold? You can't just walk into a store, ask for a half-gallon of lamp oil and then plonk down a gold ingot and wait for your change!

'Can't we just saw it into pieces?' asked Joe Short.

'That ain't going to look suspicious, is it?' replied Bob Vallence with heavy sarcasm. 'Just a bit of a gold ingot, cut off like you'd break off a piece from a candy bar? That's a right good scheme I don't think.'

'What about hammering it into little chunks, like they might be placer as we've picked up from a river bed?' suggested Wolfrider. 'Make it so it doesn't look like it's been refined at all.'

This was a relatively sensible idea and the Vallences mulled it over. They were all waiting to hear what Tom had to say about it, he being the one who would ultimately decide upon the correct course of action. He remained silent and after a while, Bob prompted him,

'What d'you say, Tom? How'd we play this?'

'We need to take this to a proper town and sell it to a jeweller or something of that sort. There's nothing like that in this pesthole, so we'll have to go across into Kansas to a big town.'

'Hell,' said Sadler, who seldom spoke unless he had something worth saying, 'we ain't got a bean between the six of us. How we going to be able to buy food or aught, to say nothing of paying for a hotel or such? We turn up in a decent town like we are now, without shaving and bathing, and I tell you now, we got 'outlaw from the territories' writ all over us. No jeweller goin' to buy no five pounds o' gold from such as us.'

Everybody watched Tom Vallence's face during this, wondering if he would serve Fenton Sadler as he had the Choctaw half-breed. He didn't. He laughed and said,

'You set the case out just right, Sadler. You're nobody's fool. We need a little stake money before crossing the border. And I'm going to tell you how we'll get it.'

There didn't seem any particular point in fretting about just why the chief of detectives from the railroad company would want to conceal his identity. Maybe, thought Grafton, men like that got into the habit of being sly and not revealing to others who they were. In any case, he didn't himself immediately announce to every stranger he met that he, Will Grafton, was a grocer. Why should he expect a detective to do so?

By the late afternoon Grafton had more or less decided to book a train heading south to Denniston in Texas; one that left the day after tomorrow. He hardly thought it likely that the Vallences would make another raid for at least forty-eight hours after their latest and successful attack. He was tired and thought that it might not be a bad notion to have a little lie-down on the bed in his hotel room.

Will Grafton collected the key from reception and went up to the second floor. The hotel was clean and comfortable, if a little spartan in its services. He unlocked the door to his room and went in. As soon as he entered the room he was grabbed roughly by one arm and hurled on to the bed. The man who had assaulted him then closed the door firmly. The menacing stranger turned to Grafton and said,

'I hear you been asking a whole heap of questions about the railroad. I think it's time that you and me had a little talk.'

CHAPTER 5

On visiting the telegraph office at midday McKinley was pleased to find a message waiting for him from his cousin, who would be arriving at two that very afternoon. He decided to meet Jacob at the station. He hadn't seen Jacob Foreman for better than two years and wondered how he would be looking. His cousin lived a tougher life than he did himself and sometimes that can take its toll on a man.

Jacob didn't look the least bit different from when he had last seen him. The big man looked a little out of place in a town like Parsons. Looking at him, ambling along the platform, you might have thought that Jacob Foreman had stepped out of a historical pageant; there was a look of Jim Bridger or Davy Crocket about him. Here was clearly a man who lived a lot of his life in the outdoors; he had a weather-beaten and travel-stained air about him. Put Jacob Foreman into a brand-new suit and cut his hair short; it would make no difference. He was a great bear of a man who belonged in the open air.

The two men embraced awkwardly. McKinley said,

'It's good to see you, man. We don't get together nearly often enough for my liking.'

'Huh,' said the other. 'It's all well and good for you to say so. I sure hope you ain't called me here on a snipe hunt. I have a busy life, not just loafing around in Pullman cars all day like some folk I could mention.'

'I think you'll say it's worth it when I show you how things stand. We stand to make a tidy sum out of this, I'm telling you.'

'I reckon,' said Jacob, 'that that all depends on what you are pleased to call a tidy sum. We'll see. Where you staying?'

The two men went on to the hotel McKinley was staying at. While his cousin was shaving and smartening himself up the telegram boy came to the lounge in search of McKinley. He had with him an urgent telegram from the directors of the Katy and when McKinley read the message, he could hardly believe his luck. He reckoned that Jake would thank his lucky stars that he had come to Parsons when he learned about this.

When Jacob came down he looked a little more human and less like some mountain man who'd never set foot in a real town. He accepted McKinley's offer of a bite to eat and the two men repaired to the restaurant.

Once the food was on the table Jacob said, 'Well? What's the case?'

'You hear about the Vallence brothers?'

The other shook his head, saying: 'I don't recollect the name. Who are they?'

'They're two-bit gunslingers from Kansas. They killed a few men up in Clay County, stole some horses and left one step ahead of a posse. Then they drifted east for a while, looting and killing as they went.'

Jake shrugged. 'So? There's a hundred men like that in every state of the union. They ain't worth chasing. You call me here for that?'

'Hold your horses 'til you hear the full story. They tried to rob a train on the Southern Pacific earlier this month. Shot and killed a woman who was in the wrong place. There were those as said that the Southern Pacific should have offered a reward after the murder and that they didn't put them in a bad light. That's as maybe.

'A few days ago the three Vallence brothers, along with four other men, held up a train in what used to be the Indian Nations. They didn't get away with a cent, but then last night they ambushed the Katy *Flyer* and made off with a couple o' thousand dollars' worth of gold bullion. A passenger was killed.'

'You're a wordy bastard, Bryan. Always were, even as a boy.'

McKinley wasn't at all put out by this. He said, 'What it is Jake, if I don't give you chapter and verse, you're not apt to understand the play.'

'Go on. Just try and finish the story this side o' Thanksgiving.'

'Well then, they hit three trains this month and two people been killed, one of them a woman. The

Southern Pacific have now got a conscience and have decided to offer a reward. They been in touch with the Katy, and between the two of them they have come up with one of the biggest rewards I ever heard tell of.'

It was clear that Jacob Foreman was interested now, because he was leaning forward eagerly, like a hungry animal who has had some juicy titbit dangled in front of his nose.

'How much?' he asked.

'Five thousand dollars for every member of the Vallence gang. Dead or alive, on identification by a sheriff or marshal. There's seven of 'em, Jake. That totals up to thirty-five thousand dollars for the whole bunch of them.'

It would be stretching the truth a little to say that there was universal and unbounded enthusiasm for Tom Vallence's idea about robbing a third train in almost as many days.

'They goin' to be waitin' for us,' predicted Fenton Sadler. 'They'll be waitin' and we'll walk right into an ambush.'

'Not a bit of it,' said Tom. 'Nobody'll expect us to hit again so soon. Besides which, you've not heard how we'll work it this time.'

'Go on,' said his brother Pat. 'What's different this time?'

'What's different is how we take the train. I'm going to ride over to Muskogee and board the passenger service by my own self. The rest of you will be waiting some few miles along the line. I'll pull the emergency halt on the train – you know, the vacuum brake. Then you fellows ride up. We'll not fool round with the express car this time. You know why? 'Cause we're going to rob the passengers for a change. We'll walk along the train, collecting everybody's pocket books, ready cash only.'

'There's sense in the plan,' said Bob. 'They have us figured as a gang who never go for passengers. If we hit a train with nothing to mark it out, they won't be expecting us to take that one. I say it'll work.'

Whenever anybody asked Jacob Foreman what he did for a living he invariably said that he was a process server or officer of the court. Both were true, as far as they went. His profession, though, had another name, one which caused a certain amount of revulsion among many people. Whatever he described himself as, however much he chased round the woodpile, even his immediate family and close friends were under no illusion at all about the fact that Foreman was a bounty hunter.

Which, of course, was why McKinley had called him in. If those bastards running the Katy wouldn't shell out reward money to one of their employees, then the capture or killing of the Vallence Gang would have to be represented to them as being the work of an independent agent.

After he had explained how the company had cheated him out of the $500 reward money just lately, McKinley asked bluntly whether or not his cousin wanted in on this. The big man smiled and said,

'For thirty-five thousand dollars? You think I'm going to miss out on that? How do'you mean to split it?'

'Fifty-fifty, right down the middle,' said McKinley firmly. 'And don't even consider trying to chisel me down Jacob, for I won't have it.'

'All right, even shares it is. But first, as the old cookbook says, catch your hare. You got any lead on these fellows?'

'That I have,' said McKinley. 'I reckon they got a spy in town, somebody who can lead us to them.' He told his cousin about the man who tried to pump him for information about which trains might be carrying valuable cargoes.

'Happen you're right about that,' said Jacob. 'I heard of such people. Hangers-on who pick up a few dollars here and there from robbers for useful tips. You think this man must have a way of getting in touch with the Vallences? Well, if so I'll soon have it out of him.'

The man who had so effortlessly thrown Will Grafton on to the bed looked to that shaken individual like somebody dressed up to play the part of a frontiersman. His shoulder length hair, the twin pistols, tooled leather boots; there was something almost affectedly archaic about the fellow's rig. Even so, he plainly meant business and Grafton thought that his best bet was to stay where he was until he could figure out the game.

Jacob Foreman looked at the little shrimp on the

bed and almost laughed out loud. The man was wearing a dark jacket and pants, he was balding, wore steel-rimmed eyeglasses and was unarmed. It wouldn't, he thought take long to find out what he knew about the Vallence gang.

'Some acquaintances of mine are a bit worried about you, friend,' said Foreman. 'You been asking such a lot of questions.'

'I don't recall asking any questions. What sort of questions?'

'About railraod trains running through the Territories.'

There was, it seemed to Grafton, only one possible explanation for this hulking brute's interest in him and concern for the questions he had been asking. He could only be a member of the band riding with the Vallences. Could he actually be one of the Vallences himself? Might he – and the thought made his blood race more quickly through his veins – might he be the very man who gunned down Carrie?

'I don't hear you tellin' me what I want to know,' said the man standing by the door. 'Let me help you with that memory of yours.'

Now according to Jacob Foreman's knowledge of how the world works, things should have gone very quickly and smoothly from that point on. He would give this little fellow a scare, maybe shake him up a bit, slap him around, and then he would spill all that he knew. Jacob walked over to the bed, reached down and grabbed hold of the fellow, dragging him to his feet.

It's never a good idea to think that the world

around you works according to a set of rules and that you can play them to your own advantage every time. Foreman could see that this man wasn't wearing a gun on his hip and, moreover, he looked a meek and unassuming type. How it should have been now was that the fellow would cry something along the lines of, 'Don't hurt me, I'll tell you all that I know.'

What actually happened was that this grey little man whipped out a short-barrelled pistol from the Lord knows where and thrust it hard into the soft part of Jacob Foreman's throat, right beneath his jaw. Then he said,

'Make one move and I'm going to blow your head clean off your shoulders. I can pull this trigger quicker than you can push me away. Or maybe you don't believe that?'

Foreman believed it all right and he froze absolutely still.

The man said, 'I'm guessing you're one of those men who tried to rob the train in Alila. You would have done better to stay at home that day.'

At the thought that he might actually be in the presence of the man who had shot his wife a bubbling, primeval rage began to surge through him. He forgot all about those passages in scripture which work to discourage private vengeance and was wondering if he would be able to restrain himself.

Some of this anger communicated to the man he was holding at gunpoint, because Jacob Foreman said hastily,

'I'm no robber, I'm looking for those men, too.' It

was slowly dawning on the bounty hunter that things had taken an unexpected and unwelcome turn.

He was also uncomfortably aware that he still had a pistol sticking in his throat and that the man holding it was seething with fury.

'Listen, why don't you put down that pistol and we can talk?'

Grafton put his left hand slowly into his jacket pocket while still maintaining the pressure on the pistol that he was holding at the other man's throat. He found what he was looking for, pulled out the metal star and held it where the other could see it.

'I'm a deputy from California,' he said. 'And what's more, I have warrants for all three of the Vallences. I wonder which of them you are?'

'I ain't one of the Vallences,' said Foreman indignantly. 'You got it all wrong. I'm a process server and I'm looking to arrest them as well.'

After putting the badge back in his pocket Will Grafton kept the gun to the man's throat and reached down to remove one of Jacob's guns from its holster. He tossed it on the bed and then repeated the operation with the second one. After doing this, he slowly moved his pistol from the other man's neck and said,

'Now explain to me just who you are.'

The conversation between Will Grafton, B.B. McKinley and Jacob Foreman was not a pleasant or an amiable one. It soon became apparent that Grafton's views and those of the other two men were pretty well irreconcilable. McKinley's first suggestion was that they all three join forces and then share the reward money three ways instead of two.

This did not work, because Grafton had not the least interest in the money. His only concern was taking the Vallence brothers back to California, where they could stand trial for his wife's murder.

'That's a piece of foolishness, begging your pardon, Mr Grafton,' said Foreman. 'One way or another, those boys are going to be hanged or shot. It can't matter a damn to you whether it happens in Kansas or California.'

But it appeared that where the Vallences were called to reckoning *did* matter to Will Grafton.

He said, 'I don't know what you men are about and, without wishing to appear rude, I don't much care. I have warrants for the three of them and I'm going to arrest them and take them west.'

McKinley muttered something under his breath that sounded very much like: *The hell you will.* Out loud, he said, 'I don't see those warrants as having much force in this state. I reckon the courts in Kansas will strike them down.'

Grafton smiled apologetically and said, 'I believe you to be quite right about that. Which is why I aim to take those men in the former Indian Nations. There's no statehood in the case there and my claim will be better than your own. Strikes me that I'm the only one of the three of us as has any official standing, that is to say is a proper lawman.'

McKinley and his cousin had learned by this time that Will Grafton was really no more than a bereaved

70

grocer who had talked his local sheriff into deputizing him. To them, he was a rank amateur who had no business muscling in on their game. Their emotions were those of two professionals who were likely to be cheated of their prey by a bungling newcomer. Their only concern was about how best to cut this annoying man out of the business. As things stood, he was bidding fair to deprive them each of $17,500.

The seven men who now constituted what the newspapers were describing as 'The Vallence Gang' were staying put in their little gully until dusk. The chances of any posse having been raised after their latest exploit were slim; but not altogether non-existent. This then was the great advantage of working the territories. Law and order were virtually absent and men like them could do pretty much as they wished.

The less attractive part of the situation was that if they *were* caught by anybody, then the chances were strongly in favour of whoever had done the catching simply hanging them on the spot, without the tiresome formality of a trial.

Having nothing better to do with their time, the boys fell to talking about their lives and what they hoped to make of them. Any outsider who had been listening to these conversations might have found them profoundly dispiriting. There wasn't one of those seven men who appeared to have any greater aim in his life than to get together enough money to sate his basest appetites.

They talked of liquor they had drunk, of what they

would drink in the future, assuming they had enough money. Then they reminisced about girls that they had been in the sack with, and each man described in salacious detail the woman of his dreams: her physical attributes and appearance.

'I mind,' said the boy who called himself Wolfrider, 'That there is a cathouse in Parsons.'

'That don't signify for you,' said Fenton Sadler with a short laugh. 'They won't have Indians in that place. They're most particular.'

'I ain't Indian,' said Wolfrider indignantly. 'Leastways, not altogether.'

'You surely ain't white,' remarked Tom Vallence. 'And what the hell kind of name is 'Wolfrider', anyways?'

'I'm with our friend here on this one,' said Pat Vallence. 'It don't seem right to forbid a man from getting down with a whore, just on account of the colour of his skin.'

Tom Vallence had had about enough of all the talk about women and liquor and decided that the time had come to make sure everybody knew his role on the morrow.

'Listen up, now,' he said, 'because tomorrow is the last train we are going to be troubling for some little while. There's too much o' that kind of thing bein' done lately and, by my reckoning, some day soon there'll be a big effort to put a stop to it. But I think one more won't hurt.'

'What we goin' to do if we ain't goin' to hit no more trains?' asked Pat Vallence. To which his brother replied:

'I have it in mind that we'll wake 'em up a bit in Parsons; once we sold our gold, that is.'

'So how do we play it once you're on the train?' asked Bob.

'You boys are to be waiting right where we stole that red lantern. You mind where I mean, that little way halt?'

'Jesus, Joseph and Mary,' said Sadler. 'You ain't fixin' to rob another train in the self-same place as we did a couple o' days back? That's takin' a rare old risk.'

Tom looked at the man contemptuously, saying, 'You in or out? Just say the word and you can leave right now.'

'No, I'm in,' muttered Sadler, but he didn't look any too happy about it.

'You fellows don't need to hide or aught. I'll engage to bring the train to a halt and then you all swarm on and work your way through the passengers. We only want money. You can tell by lookin', oft-times who's worth shaking down. And don't you bastards forget to bring my mount along, neither.'

CHAPTER 6

B.B. McKinley and his cousin parted from Will Grafton on outwardly amiable terms, but within, the pair were furious. It was tolerably plain to them both that this idiot would queer the pitch for their own plans. He would try to apprehend the gang of robbers, most likely get killed in the process and who knew what would happen as a consequence. The Vallences might just light out of the territories to the Lord knew where.

They were perfectly situated as things stood for two determined men to strike them hard and bring either them or their lifeless corpses back to Parsons to be certified by the sheriff there. Then it was simply a matter of picking up the $35,000 and dividing it between them.

McKinley hinted to his cousin that with so much at stake it might be worth arranging for the widowed grocer from Alila to have some kind of accident; not a fatal one but just something which would put him out of commission for a spell, but Jacob Foreman wouldn't entertain the notion for a moment.

His objections were practical, rather than strictly ethical. Grafton was an officially appointed lawman and, in his line of work, Foreman couldn't risk being suspected of interfering with or obstructing such a person. He had his future livelihood to consider and he always took good care to stay on the right side of all law enforcement agencies, even a piddling little outfit like that in Alila.

'Is there some way that you can detain the fellow here in town for a while?' he asked his cousin. 'Not by rough stuff, mind.'

McKinley thought about it and then said, 'Lord, we're both getting silly in our old age. Of course I can stop him leaving town.'

'How's that?'

'The poor sap don't ride a horse, you know. He only goes by railroad. I'm chief of detectives for that railroad. I'll just tell the station here that he's barred from travelling on the Katy. I don't need to give any reason, my word's law about such things. I'll hint he's a fraud or card-sharper or something.'

'I should think you just about hit upon it, cousin. Meantime, I'll head down into the Indian Nations first thing tomorrow and see what's what.'

'You goin' on your own?' asked McKinley in surprise. 'There seven o' those boys, you know.'

'Don't teach your grandmother to suck eggs,' said Jacob Foreman. 'I know what I'm about. You're sure that reward is "dead or alive", I suppose?'

By which McKinley understood that his cousin was not intending even to attempt the arrest of the

Vallence gang, but would most likely try and kill them at a distance. He didn't know how bounty hunters worked and nor did he wish to. It was enough for him that cousin Jacob was regarded with some awe by all who knew of his activities in that field and that if anybody could take those rascals, then Jacob Foreman was the man for the job.

The first that Will Grafton knew of the plots being laid against him by the chief of detectives and his cousin was when he went down to the railroad station to buy a ticket for the train from Junction City to Denniston, which would be stopping at Parsons at ten the next morning. His request for a ticket was not acceded to immediately; instead, the clerk went into a back room and was gone some little while. When he returned, he was accompanied by the station master, who told him briskly,

'Sorry sir, can't be done. You ain't a-travelling on this line again.'

'Not travelling on this line,' said Grafton in amazement. 'Why, whatever can you mean? I came up from Texas by this line without any sort of difficulty.'

'That's as may be,' said the man stiffly. 'But my instructions are that you are no longer welcome on the Missouri, Kansas and Texas line. I'm sorry, but there it is.'

On hearing the word, 'instructions', everything became clear to Grafton. He said,

'And I'm guessing that these "instructions" come from B.B. McKinley; am I right?'

'I'm not answerable to you,' said the station master

shortly. 'You ain't travelling with us again and there's an end to it.'

Now being a completely law-abiding individual, this flat declaration put Grafton into something of a quandary. He didn't doubt that there were ways of riding the railroad without buying a ticket, but it wasn't a thing he ever could have imagined himself doing. Instead, he hunted out McKinley at his hotel and asked him what was going on.

'What's going on, Mr Grafton,' explained the chief of detectives, 'is that you are not going to cut me out of seventeen and a half thousand dollars, to put things bluntly.'

'Suppose I go to your employers, tell them what you're about?'

'They've heard a hundred crooks and bunco artists complain about me, tell lies and such. You go right ahead. I'm telling you now, though, you are not riding the Katy.'

And that was that; there was little to be done about the matter. Grafton was utterly baffled and B.B. McKinley and his cousin were pretty pleased with themselves.

At a few minutes before ten the next morning, Passenger Train No 1 pulled into the depot at Parsons. Waiting for it on the platform were Jacob Foreman and his cousin.

McKinley said, 'You sure you can handle this alone, Jacob? I feel kind of mean letting you do all the dangerous work and then getting the same as you.'

'Don't be a damned fool,' his cousin told him gruffly. 'You set the game up and made it possible. I wouldn't o' had an inkling about this, had it not been for you. Anyways, let's see how many of those pigeons I can hit before we count up our profits.'

'So you truly don't want me to come along?'

'You'd get in the way and likely screw things up for me,' his cousin said bluntly. 'You got your role, same as I got mine. And listen: keep a good eye on that grocer. I think there's more to him than meets the eye. I get the feeling that he'll cause us grief afore this is over.'

'Grafton?' said McKinley in surprise. 'He's a nobody. I warned him off good; we can leave him out of the reckoning entirely.'

His cousin shook his head. 'You weren't there to see how quick he pulled that gun on me. I can handle myself in most any company, but he took me by surprise. Thought he was goin' to kill me. You mind what I tell you now and set a watch upon him.'

It would be a few hours yet before the train arrived at Muskogee, but Tom Vallence wanted to be sure that he didn't miss it. His brother Bob had ridden with him to about a mile from Muskogee, where Tom had dismounted and entrusted his horse to his brother.

He said, 'Bob, you make sure that those others are right there on time. I don't aim for to stop that train and then find as it's only me robbing it all by my own self. You hear what I say?'

'It'll be all right, don't you fret none. We'll all be there, ready and waiting. You say that we should just haul aboard and start looting from the passengers as soon as it stops?'

'Yeah, that's about the strength of it. And have an eye on that half-breed. I don't trust him. He's got a treacherous look about him.'

'Ah, he's not a bad fellow. Not once you get used to his ways. Him and you, the two o' you just seem to rub each other up the wrong way.'

Now although neither man knew it, the stage was already set for problems, because of a trifling little omission on the part of Tom Vallence. In all the talk of the others swarming on board and robbing the passengers, he hadn't thought it necessary to mention that one man at least would have to stay and cover the driver and fireman, to make sure that they behaved themselves and didn't start the locomotive rolling or anything of that nature. He'd taken it as read that such a precaution would be necessary and it slipped his mind to underline the importance of ensuring that the train was immobilized for the duration of their robbery.

Muskogee was, in Tom Vallence's considered and unbiased opinion, the most dead-and-alive shithole he had encountered in the whole of his short life. There were two little stores, a saloon that might hold a dozen men at a pinch and a collection of small, single-storey buildings; some of them were soddies and some looked like they had been thrown together from unseasoned timber. Tom figured that most people in these parts, that is to say those who had homesteaded into this district last year, lived scattered about at varying distances from this little pesthole. How the hell was he going to pass two or three hours here?

Anybody looking at Jacob Foreman, as he sprawled at his ease in a window seat on Passenger Train No. 1 of the Missouri, Kansas and Texas railroad line, would probably not have pegged him for a bounty hunter. His appearance was rather that of a very rough and ready settler from out West. The two pistols might have raised eyebrows; after all, most men got by quite happily with one.

However, it was by no means unknown for eccentric men and show-offs to sport a couple of guns in that way. Anybody looking inside the battered old carpet-bag resting in the seat next to him, though, might have drawn in their breath sharply, because it contained the most extraordinary weapon you were ever likely to see.

Jacob Foreman might try to conceal his true calling by introducing himself as a process server or court official, but even so, there were a number of people who penetrated these euphemisms and concluded that he was a bounty hunter. Even that grim title did not fully do justice to his profession. It would have been more accurate to call the man a bounty *killer*, because it was a rare occasion indeed when Foreman brought his quarry in alive.

Very early on in his career McKinley's cousin had realized that there was no percentage at all in bringing men in alive if he would be paid precisely the same for them just on production of a dead body. Try and transport a living, vicious, cunning and homicidal bandit a hundred miles and you are looking at a difficult and dangerous job. Turn that same man into a corpse and you can just sling him over a horse and lead him behind you. It was this inescapable logic that dictated Jacob Foreman's *modus operandi*.

An inevitable corollary of the practice of killing fugitives before bringing them in, was that it was far better, if your own safety and well-being were paramount and you were in any case going to kill somebody, to shoot the man at a goodly distance, rather than engaging in a duel or other type of fair fight. As a result of much cogitating on this question, Foreman had devised an ingenious weapon, which he used as soon as he had positively identified his prey. He carried the pieces of this singular device dismantled in an old carpetbag. It certainly looked more innocuous than carrying a hunting rifle or scattergun under his arm all the time.

Sitting in his hotel room in Parsons, Grafton dashed off a few lines to his children. He wrote:

Dear children,
Just a few lines to let you know that I have not forgotten you. Things have not lately gone as I could have wished, but as I have told you all more than once, we must meet our reverses boldly and not give up. I know where the bad men who hurt your Mama are hiding and as soon as I am able to get there, I am going to invite them to accompany me back to Alila. Not everybody wants to

help and so I have had to speak my mind plainly to one or two folk. I hope that you are all minding what your Aunt Martha tells you and not making a fuss about having baths and going to bed when you are told. This is particularly directed at Billy-Joe and Linton; I know that you, Ella, are not so opposed to bathing and going to bed as are your brothers. I hope to have this business cleared up in a few days and then I shall hurry home to you all.

Your loving Pa.

After he had completed this letter Will Grafton sat for a while, thinking about Carrie. It seemed to him that his life had been as dry as dust until Caroline Paxton, as she then was, came into it. He could picture her now, a bright, lively girl of twenty and he a serious and rather dull man of forty. It had been a strange chance that threw them together, but they had enjoyed a blessed twelve years and at least he had the children to remember her by. The grief of her death was still there, but he had put it aside until a due season in which he could indulge it.

The important thing for now was to run those villains to earth and take them back to face justice. It was a pity that that foolish fellow who worked for the railroad had set himself in opposition to Grafton's interests. The love of money was a terrible thing and Grafton half wished he had brought with him a supply of the printed tracts which he kept on the counter of his shop for anybody as wanted one.

At this thought, he half smiled. He had an idea that McKinley and that strange-looking relative of his were not the kind to be swayed by a passage from scripture.

Grafton decided to take the letter to the mail. He sealed it in an envelope, addressed it and then went out into the streets. As he walked along he wondered if he ought to acquire a horse and make his way south on that. It took only a few seconds to persuade himself of the folly of such a course of action. He knew almost nothing at all about the care of horses and even if he could stay on the beast, he had an idea it would make for slow travelling indeed. No, for the time being he would, perforce, remain here in Parsons and hope that some new development would chance which would bring him closer to the men he sought.

In fact, before the week was out, he and the Vallence gang would be set directly on a collision course, but of that Will Grafton had not the slightest premonition.

After two hours in Muskogee Tom Vallence was going almost out of his mind with boredom. It might not have been so bad if he had had even enough money to visit the saloon and have a drink or two, but until they fleeced the passengers of the next train through he was utterly destitute. It was mad; he had eighty ounces of fine gold to his name and couldn't even buy a whiskey!

He could not for the life of him imagine how those living round here could bear their existence. It had been bad enough in the little town where he had grown up, but Carville was like a mighty metropolis compared to this place. He walked up and down the main and only street, restlessly prowling backwards and forwards like a caged tiger. Gradually the morning wore away until he heard in the distance the whistle of the approaching train.

There were two other passengers waiting by the wooden sign that indicated that the train should stop there. One was an old party: a woman of about seventy or eighty years of age by the look of it. The other was a farmer, probably one of those who had moved in last year when the territory was opened up.

Tom took a seat at the back of the very last coach. As he boarded he had made a note of where the handle operating the emergency brake was situated and had sat right beneath it, an ornate, wrought-iron pull, with a sign warning of the dire penalties attached to using it without proper need. He would be able to reach up and pull the thing without hardly raising himself from his seat. He had no idea of how it worked, but he knew that the train would come to a halt very swiftly once the emergency handle had been operated.

The question was, how long would it take to stop? Presumably, it would be a lot sharper and quicker than the gentle slowing down which took place when a railroad train came to a rest at a station. He figured that if he gave it half a mile, he would be gauging it pretty much right. He just hoped that those men of his would be ready to ride forward smartly if he had misjudged the distance. He would have to rely on Bob and Pat to see to that.

A voice behind him said, 'Excuse me, young man, would you mind lifting my bag up into that there overhead rack?'

He looked round and saw the old woman who had also been waiting for the train at Muskogee.

'Why surely, ma'am,' he said and stood to lift the little bag up and on to the netting of the rack.

'Thank you kindly,' said the woman. 'I never like to leave my bag on a seat, in case it gets stolen, you know.'

So comical was the situation, with this trusting old person asking a seasoned robber to lift her bag up to keep it safe from theft, that Tom Vallence almost burst out laughing. Instead, he grunted and sat back down again. He was prodded gently from behind.

'I'm seventy-eight,' announced the old woman, the way that somebody might boast of a specially good hand at poker. 'I'm going to meet my daughter and her family in Austin. In Texas, you know.'

Despite his rough nature, Tom felt unable to snub this poor old soul, so he turned and said politely,

'I hope you have a right good visit, ma'am.'

'Visit? I ain't a-going to visit, I'm moving there to live with them.'

Now even the most ruthless bandit cannot always be drinking, cursing, shooting and killing, and there was something so pleasant and mild about this woman that Tom began listening to her in earnest and offering the occasional comment to encourage her flow of conversation. Something about her reminded him of his own grandmama, who had been dead these ten years.

It will scarcely be credited, but so engrossed did he

become with talking to Mrs Lefay, as she had introduced herself, that he was suddenly aware that the train was almost at the spot where his brothers and the other three men would be waiting for him. He half-rose from his seat, stretched up and pulled the handle of the vacuum brake.

'He's leaving it damned late to yank that brake,' observed Pat Vallence to his brother, as he pulled the neckerchief up and over the lower half of his face. 'That train goin' to shoot by us at this rate.'

Bob looked anxiously at the oncoming locomotive and said uncertainly, 'I mind Tom knows what's best.' Even so, he, like his brother, had had a sudden feeling of unease. It wasn't just the train not slowing down; there was something he couldn't rightly put his finger on, a sense that things were going wrong.

Bob Vallence was struggling to work out how to put this into words for his brother. They were neither of them great ones for talking, and finding the right words for a complicated concept of this sort took a little thinking about.

He had just put his thoughts in order and was ready to tell his brother what he meant, when the man on the other side of him from his brother, Fenton Sadler, jerked back in his saddle with half of his head shot away. A fraction of a second later came the crack of a rifle shot.

CHAPTER 7

The man in the seat across the aisle from Jacob Foreman had made one or two desultory attempts to lure him into conversation, but the bounty hunter was not so human as Tom Vallence. He didn't give a good goddamn about this stranger's life history and made it perfectly obvious that he wasn't going to so much as open his mouth in response to the other's overtures. In a business of this kind you couldn't lower your guard for a single second. He had no particular present expectation of being bushwhacked, but on the other hand, given recent events, it was a distinct possibility.

That being so, he did not take his eyes off the surrounding countryside for a moment. So it was that he was aware before anybody else on the train, even the driver, that a group of riders were hanging about some three-quarters of a mile ahead of them. He couldn't be sure at this point that they were possessed of evil designs regarding the train upon which he was travelling, but he surely was not about to take any chances. Foreman opened the carpetbag on the seat besides him, opened it up and began removing the contents.

Not long after he had picked up as a bounty hunter Jacob Foreman had realized that he would need something pretty special in the way of weaponry. True, the two capable forty-fives which he carried at his hips would answer well enough for close-quarters work, but then again, one didn't always wish to engage in gunplay of that sort, where there was a very real risk of being killed. Far better to take your man at a good, long distance, before he was even aware that he was the object of your hostile interest.

There were five components in the carpetbag, the longest of which was an eighteen-inch-long metal tube with a screw thread at one end. In addition to this were what looked like half a pistol without the wooden grips, two other metal tubes, one of them made of brass and of a strange triangular shape, seemingly formed by bending a strip of metal into something resembling part of a skeleton.

It took the bounty hunter less than five seconds to screw the long tube into the pistol mechanism and snap the other parts into place. Having done so, he was holding in his hands the strangest-looking rifle imaginable.

Jacob Foreman's rifle was made up of various parts of a Winchester, combined with bits and pieces from other weapons. The skeleton stock, he had had a blacksmith forge for him, and the brass tube, which ran along the top of the barrel, was the telescopic sight from a British Whitworth rifle. He opened the window and could see at once that the riders were all pulling on masks; there could be not the slightest doubt that they were planning to hold up the train upon which he was travelling.

Foreman poked the barrel of his extraordinary firearm through the window and rested it on the frame. Then he cocked his piece, squinted down the sight and took careful aim at the chest of one of the riders, who was by this time only 400 yards or so ahead of him.

Some men favoured head shots, with the near certainty of death for the victim, but when you are hoping to collect money on a corpse this isn't the smart move. Sheriffs' offices are always on the lookout for ways to avoid paying out on rewards, and some dead man without a face is the perfect opportunity to deny that in life this man really was a wanted outlaw.

No, a rifle bullet in the chest will do the job just as neatly; always providing that you are able to place your shot in the middle of the chest. McKinley's cousin had had long practice at this, and as he squeezed the trigger he could see the cross hairs smack bang in the centre of the breast of one of the riders.

As Foreman fired his shot two things happened in quick succession. The first was that the driver of the train applied his brakes suddenly and violently. This caused the bounty hunter's shot to go wide, although in the event it still killed the intended target. That was a minor irritation compared with what happened next, because the unexpected jerk caused him to lose hold of his precious rifle and, to his dismay, it was precipitated out of the window.

As soon as the train began braking Jacob Foreman's mind was racing ahead, trying to work out what was happening. You don't survive for years in that trade without an ability to think very swiftly in an emergency. By the time he had fired that shot and the rifle had been shaken from his hand he knew exactly what the score was. There was no reason for the driver of the train to apply his brakes just because he saw a bunch of armed men ahead. Quite the opposite, in fact; you'd think that he would speed up, rather than stop.

No, the answer was that somebody on this train had pulled the emergency handle to bring the train to a halt. In other words, the bandits out there had an accomplice on the train. The thought was no sooner completed than the train sailed past the waiting riders and came to a stop 200 yards beyond them.

Tom Vallence was cursing himself quietly and calling himself all manner of uncomplimentary names. He knew that he had screwed up badly, because at the very same instant that he had pulled that handle he had heard a shot come from down the end of the coach.

Worse than that though, was seeing his partners as he swept past them and the dawning realization that things were going badly wrong. Behind him, he could hear old Mrs Lefay saying anxiously:

'Oh my, whatever's wrong? Why did you pull the brake like that?'

Without answering Vallence pulled out his pistol and peered round the seats, trying to see who had been shooting. Whoever it had been, he would have to deal with that individual before he and his comrades settled down to looting the train.

The five surviving members of the party galloped after the train as it raced past them. To be strictly accurate, four of them galloped, while Bob Vallence, who was encumbered by his brother Tom's horse as well, proceded more at a cross between a trot and a canter. Controlling two horses at once at speed is very much an acquired skill and this was the first time that Bob Vallence had ever been called upon to perform such a feat.

It is hardly necessary to mention that as soon as they caught up with Passenger Train No. 1, which had now ground to a halt, the five men leaped from their horses and scrambled up into the last coach, with not one of them having time to give the least thought to any ideas that the driver or fireman might be having.

The bounty hunter had drawn one of his pistols and was looking round warily to see if he could guess who had signalled for the train to stop. He and Tom Vallence both stood up at precisely the same moment and both guessed at that moment that here was an enemy.

Jacob Foreman was quicker than 'most anybody in that part of the country at aiming and shooting a pistol; he had to be, his very life depended upon it. Even so, it might have been a dead heat; Tom Vallence too was mighty fast. He had a handicap though, in that the old woman sitting behind him cried out in a piercing and querulous voice, when she saw Vallence's gun,

'Help, murder!' The distraction was sufficient to

delay his shot and allow his adversary to fire first.

In the usual way of things Tom Vallence would have been killed on the spot by that first shot of the bounty hunter's, had it not been for that individual having his aim spoiled for the second time that day by the driver of Passenger Train No 1, who this time started the train moving without any warning and nearly caused Jacob Foreman to fall over. His first shot went wild, giving Vallence the opportunity to fire back and then duck for cover behind the seat in front of him.

By this time his brothers and the other two had opened the door behind him at the end of the coach. Seeing somebody shooting in their direction, they began vigorously returning fire. Tom Vallence said to Bob and Pat,

'That bastard driver has started moving again. We got to get up to the front and stop him.'

Foreman had seen the bandits boarding the train behind the other gunman and did not feel inclined to take on five men at once at close quarters. He dropped to the floor and began crawling along beneath the seats on his hands and knees. Experience had taught him to suppose that once he had disappeared from sight it would be at least half a minute before anybody risked coming to where he had last been seen.

The need to get the train stopped again was becoming more desperate with every passing second. It was the young half-breed who solved the problem, although to his own detriment. He went haring up the coach, gun in hand, intending to race the whole length of the train, then put a gun to the head of the driver and force him to apply the brakes.

As he ran past Jacob Foreman the bounty hunter took his chance and jumped up, firing twice into the Choctaw's back. He would have done better to stay low, because the instant he betrayed his position, Tom and Bob Vallence shot him simultaneously. One bullet struck his right shoulder and the other caught his head a glancing blow, sending him staggering into the aisle so that he was in plain view of the four men at the end of the coach. They all fired repeatedly at him.

'Bob,' said Tom Vallence, 'get down after that damned driver at once. Get him to halt and then back up. You two help me collect up the money.'

Once Bob had gone running off to the front of the train Tom Vallence called out, saying,

'Any man or woman who opposes us, I'm a-goin' to shoot that person down like a mangy dog. Anybody who don't hand over his money, I'm goin' to kill him. You seen we ain't foolin' now.'

None of the passengers offered any resistance as the three men walked down the aisle, inviting them to throw their cash into a leather saddle-bag held invitingly open by Pat Vallence.

The passengers in the other carriages through which Bob passed on his way to the locomotive, had worked out by now that a robbery was in progress. All of them pointedly looked out of the window as the man with a gun in his hand sprinted past. Nobody felt like being heroic that day.

When he reached the last coach Bob Vallence opened the door and found himself confronted by the coal tender. He knew he'd need both hands for this, so he holstered his pistol and jumped up, catching on to the edge of the tender with his fingertips. Then he pulled himself up by main force until he was crouched on the pile of coal. You could accuse the Vallence brothers of a whole heap of terrible things, but nobody ever suggested that any of them lacked courage.

Bob scrambled across the coal. When he was in sight of the cab of the locomotive, he drew his gun again and fired at the roof of the cab. The bullet ricocheted off the metal, causing the driver and fireman to turn round in alarm. When they saw the bandit crouched behind them they thought it was all up with them. Bob shouted, his voice just audible above the sound of the steam engine and the hissing of the wind.

'Apply those brakes or I will kill the two of you.'

There was no reason to doubt that the threat was meant sincerely, so the driver carefully slowed down and after a while brought the locomotive to a halt. They could hear Bob Vallence's next instruction more clearly, now that they were stationary.

He said, 'Now back up, slowly and be ready to stop when I say.'

Very carefully and slowly the train began to move backwards along the track.

As Tom Vallence passed the supine figure of the bounty hunter he aimed a vicious kick at the dead man's face, muttering, 'Whoreson!' as he did so. He glanced from the window and was relieved to see that the horses had not wandered too far from the train and would not take too much catching. The train stopped and his brother Bob came sauntering towards him.

'I told that driver that if he moves this pile of iron an inch before we are all mounted and on our way I will go back and kill him,' said Bob Vallence. 'From the look on his face, I guess he took me at my word.'

'We best dig up,' said Tom. 'The half-breed's dead, which I'm sorry about. He gave us our chance to get that dog who was shooting at us. There's just the four of us. Let's go.'

Tom Vallence was a cold-hearted man and one not given to displays of emotion. Nevertheless, something happened as they were about to leave that train that moved him almost to tears. As they walked to the rear of the final coach Pat touched his arm and said,

'We didn't notice that, in all the excitement.' Tom looked to where his brother pointed and saw to his horror that the old woman whom he had been chatting to was sitting there in her seat, stone dead. A bullet had passed through her left eye and into her brain. He stopped dead in his tracks and said softly;

'Ah, that's the hell of a thing to happen. Her name was Mrs Lefay and she was goin' to live in Austin.' He stood there for a moment, unaccountably grief-stricken at the death of this stranger.

'She was shot from the front,' said Pat, practically. 'Must have been a bullet from that fellow as was shooting at us. We didn't kill her.'

'Yeah, we did,' said Tom. 'We hadn't o' been robbing this train, she'd still be alive.' Then he shook himself and said, 'All right, let's be going, afore we get a posse on our tail.'

The robbery of Passenger Train No 1 and the brutal slaying of two passengers as well as the deaths of two of the outlaws was the theme of general conversation in Parsons a few days later. The directors of the Missouri, Kansas and Texas Railroad Company were not at all happy with their chief of detectives, believing that he was falling down on the job by not preventing these depredations against their trains. Sales of tickets were plummeting and, in an even more disturbing develop-ment, valuables were being sent by stage rather than by rail. This struck at a major source of income for the Katy and they were becoming altogether distracted by the situation.

B.B. McKinley was sorry to hear about his cousin's death, but a sight sorrier not to have the benefit of that $17,500 which he had been counting on. McKinley's creditors were becoming very restless and pressing him more every day for payment. He was beginning to turn his mind to a variety of increasingly frantic and outlandish schemes for getting straight on the finan-cial front.

The news of the latest outrage came as little or no surprise to Will Grafton. That an accomplished bounty hunter had been unable to capture the Vallence brothers was not startling news to the grocer. Ever since he had heard about Tom Vallence managing to escape from not one but two deputies, Grafton had known that if those men were brought to book, he would probably have to undertake the task himself.

The old saying about needing to do a job oneself if one wanted it to be done properly was often on his lips during his day-to-day work at the store. He didn't see that the case would be all that different if it came to catching killers. There was no point trusting others to do it for you. Whether it was checking an invoice for sacks of corn or capturing train robbers and taking them to jail, the principle was precisely the same.

Three days after the terrible events surrounding Passenger Train No 1 Will Grafton chanced to bump into McKinley while walking along Main Street. He raised his hat to the chief of detectives and said,

'My condolences for your cousin, Mr McKinley. I hardly knew him, but he seemed like a decent fellow.'

McKinley couldn't make out whether or not the grocer was taunting him or being sincere. He said,

'Just what are you still doing here? You know you ain't goin' to get down into the Territories and in any case, that gang are probably in Mexico by now.'

'Oh, I wouldn't have thought so,' said Grafton. 'Whatever would they do in a foreign country? No, they're lying low. You can bet that various posses have been out hunting them and that they'll be moving somewhere else soon, but it won't be Mexico. I'm thinking that they will come this way. I think you did me a favour, Mr McKinLey, by not letting me go flying off to the Indian Nations.'

Talking to Grafton was, decided the chief of detectives, a mighty wearisome occupation. He could not make out whether the man was as sharp as a lancet or a complete damned fool.

He said, 'Mr Grafton, suppose I were to rescind my prohibition on you travelling on the Katy? Wouldn't you just like to get back home to California and forget all this nonsense?'

'It's very kind of you, Mr McKinley, but I couldn't think of it. When I say I'll do a thing, then it will be done. It's like our Lord said, when a man puts his hand to the plough, he should never look back. You read scripture, perhaps?'

'No, I can't say as I do. I haven't time for such foolishness.'

'Well, you miss out on an awful lot. It's been nice chatting to you, but I have a lot to do. Good day to you, Mr McKinley.'

After the grocer had left B.B. McKinley stood staring after him as he walked down the street to wherever he was going. The detective recollected what his cousin had said about the fellow. Jacob was scared of nobody and was generally unimpressed by the worst villains, but there had been something about that Will Grafton that had given him pause. Could it really be that he was a singular person and not the hopeless case he appeared to McKinley's eyes?

Grafton had not wasted the last three days. He'd bought a large-scale map of the area surrounding Parsons and had been thinking a lot about the possible courses open to the Vallence brothers. The more he thought about it, the more likely he thought it was that the brothers and whatever poor fools they had dragged into their gang would be heading north.

He understood from the newspaper reports that they hailed from Clay County, which was, according to his map, right up in the north-east corner of the state. They had seemingly got good reason to give that district a wide berth, but they were surely unknown in the rest of Kansas? Texas was a rough place and they would be working there in competition with some pretty fierce types, who might not be over pleased to see a new gang trying to gouge a share of the profits from robbery there. Kansas, on the other hand, was relatively quiet these days and there would be more scope for banditry.

It had been many years since he had gambled so much as a cent, but had Grafton been a betting man, then he would have put all his money on the three Vallence brothers fetching up in Kansas before too long.

McKinley's office was up in Junction City, but since that was where many of the people to whom he owed money were also to be found, he was in no great hurry to go back there. Not but that he didn't owe a good deal down here as well, which necessitated a bit of ducking out of the way when he caught sight of certain individuals walking down the street towards him, but Parsons was a better place to be right now. For one thing, his bosses wanted him on the case of the train robbers and he could give a greater impression of industry as 'the man on the spot' if he wasn't sitting in his Junction City office.

The reward money for the Vallences still looked to

be the best way that McKinley had of balancing his books and it had been a cruel blow when his cousin's efforts had come to naught. Still, that was the way of the world and there was no point fretting unduly about such misfortunes. The question was: what was to be done about it? Was it still possible to get that money?

It had been a rough and tiring week. They had known fine well that the whole entire area within miles of that train would soon be covered with riders trying to seek them out, so the Vallences had ridden hard to be clear of the storm. They found shelter in the most surprising place when they stumbled across a Creek village. The village elder or chief or whatever you could call such a man, had spoken to them. He knew, and they never figured out how, that they were wanted bandits. He asked no foolish questions but at once offered to show them a cave up in the side of a nearby hill, where they could stay. He even offered to have food and water sent up each day to them.

Tom Vallence, a man who took a dim view of ideas such as altruism and compassion, brooded over this apparent kindness until he came up with the answer. It couldn't be that the Creek were scared of them. There were dozens of strong young men in the village, armed to the teeth and probably not at all keen on white men. They could have dispatched the four strangers in no time at all had they been minded to do so.

After a lot of hard thinking Tom Vallence came up with what was probably the correct solution to the puzzle. It was simply that the Creek were angry about the way that the white men had torn up their treaties and seized this whole territory last year. They figured that those like the Vallences who created a lawless and wild atmosphere in the former Indian Nations would act to discourage further settlers from moving in.

There was an old Creek saying: *The enemy of my enemy is my friend.* As long as men like the Vallences were fighting the forces of law and order, the Creek would cheerfully lend them a hand where they could.

Tom, Bob and Pat Vallence had much lively, and at times almost violent, discussion about where they ought next to head. Joe Short, the surviving member of those who had been riding with the Vallences, felt himself to be in a minority and thought it wisest to keep his mouth closed.

'We ain't goin' down to Texas,' announced Tom, 'and that's flat. The place is crawling with men like us, there's too much competition. No, I got a better idea.'

'If'n this tends towards us going back to Kansas,' said Pat, 'then I say no. We goin' to get our necks stretched, we ain't careful.'

'Tom ain't suggesting going back to Clay County, nor anywhere near it,' Bob said, hoping to smooth over any dissent. 'That's right Tom, isn't it?'

'Hell, yeah,' said his brother, giving a short laugh. 'I'm no keener on being hanged than the next man. I'm talkin' about Parsons.'

'Parsons?' said Pat. 'What the hell's Parsons got to do with anything?'

Tom Vallence thought it time to set out his stall and

to explain to his slower-witted brother the advantages that would accrue to them from spending a day or two in the town of Parsons.

CHAPTER 8

Jacob Foreman was not the only bounty hunter who had had his eye on the territories. By now the reward being offered by the Southern Pacific and Missouri, Kansas and Texas railroads was common knowledge and a number of men who thought that they might be able to catch the brothers had arrived in Parsons, the obvious jumping-off spot for a foray into the former Indian Nations.

McKinley faced two problems. First off, of course, he had to select a man he could trust to share that reward money with him. Next was where he had to provide his chosen confederate with a motive for giving half of the proceeds of his enterprise to the chief of detectives for the Katy.

On the face of it there was no special reason for anybody to do so. Those men who made a living through collecting reward money generally worked alone, for the very reason that they were greedy and unscrupulous individuals who wanted any money floating around to come exclusively to them.

While wrestling with this puzzle McKinley still kept seeing Will Grafton about town. The grocer was always very polite to him, raising his hat and asking how things were going, but the chief of detectives was still uneasy about the fellow. He was just too mild-mannered and quiet to be true. He recalled again what his cousin had told him, that Grafton had got the drop on the bounty hunter and that Jacob had been in fear of his life. B. B. McKinley prided himself on being a good judge of men and something here didn't tally up. He liked to be able to put men into neat little compartments and the grocer didn't fit into any category that McKinley could think of.

Will Grafton was a modest man, who always underestimated his own abilities. This was part of his charm to those who associated with him in Alila. He was never bumptious or pushy and only put forward his own ideas with the greatest reluctance, as though expecting to have them dismissed out of hand by others. This was not affectation, but rather the genuine humility of a man who doubts that he is any smarter or shrewder than his neighbours. Nevertheless, he was puzzled right now by what he saw as a lack of foresight in the men concerned with tracking down the Vallence brothers.

Could it really be that he, Will Grafton, was the only person to recollect the five gold ingots that those men had stolen from the express car so recently? Surely not? Although he had, in the past, worked for the Provost Marshal's office and had even, indeed, attained the rank of provost marshal himself, it must be the case that modern law-enforcement agents knew more than he about how things worked today? Was he missing something?

It was plain as a pikestaff to the grocer that the men who had stolen that gold would have to leave the territories if they wanted to sell it for anything near its true value. They might find some crooked man who would take it off their hands for a fraction of its value, but if they wanted to get twenty dollars or more an ounce for it, they would be obliged to come to a decent-sized town and then find a jeweller who bought and sold gold.

All this was so obvious to Will Grafton that he knew the best move he could make right now was no move at all. He had no doubt at all that if he sat tight and bided his time those boys would fetch up in Parsons soon. The territories were too hot for them after all their banditry, and they might be looking for another source of income before too long.

'I don't aim to be running and hiding for much longer,' said Tom Vallence as he and the others sat in the cave above the Creek village. 'I'm strongly minded to settle down a little, find a farm or some such.'

'A farm?' said Pat, intrigued at this new development. 'You want we should get up like Pa at dawn and break our backs planting corn and grubbing in the dirt? I don't take to that notion, nohow!'

'Who said aught about digging and planting, you

105

noodle,' replied his brother irritably. 'I'm talkin' 'bout somewhere to live that ain't in a town with a heap of nosy neighbours.'

'There's something in that,' said Bob Vallence slowly. 'Meaning that we could live quietly, 'cept when we was out on the scout?'

'That's the strength of it. We could have us a base. Maybe keep horses, buyin' and selling them, too.' Tom didn't spell it out in as many words, but the others took him to mean by this that the animals they would be buying and selling would not be honestly acquired. After spending a few days up in this cave, the notion of a permanent base was an attractive one, and Pat came round as well to the Parsons plan.

Joe Short was feeling left out of this conversation, just as he had done in practically all the other talk since they arrived at the Creek village. He wondered where, if at all, he would fit into these plans being hatched by the Vallences.

Asking around the saloons and cathouses in Parsons, it didn't take B.B. McKinley too long to come up with the names of one or two likely candidates for becoming his partner. Not every drifter passing through town was a bounty hunter, of course, but his years of experience had given McKinley a cat's sense for those of that brand.

He had decided what his line would be, the hook that would lure a man to throw in his lot with an official of the railroad. He would claim that the directors of the Katy were notorious for reneging on their offers and that in return for a third share of the reward money, he would expedite the claim and see that they received the full amount.

It sounded a little thin, even to him, but there it was; that was the best that he could come up with. It would mean too, dropping his share by $5,000, but he really didn't see any percentage in being too greedy: $12,500 might be less than $17,500 but both sums were vast improvements on nothing.

The first man he approached laughed in his face.

'You say what?' he exclaimed incredulously when McKinley had broached the subject to him in the Lucky Horseshoe. 'You think I'm a-goin' to share the money with you? Point one is where your figuring is way out, anyway. There ain't no seven members of that gang any more, it's down to four.

'Next, I can claim a reward well enough without some mealy-mouthed detective acting as my mouth-piece.

'Last off is where you don't look like a man I would trust to keep a-hold o' my horse while I was taking a leak, never mind represent me in an affair involvin' thousands of dollars.'

It was fortunate for McKinley that he had a thick skin, because the response of the other men he approached were pretty much the same, although some were even less complimentary about him and his proposal.

He was beginning to become seriously worried, because one man to whom he owed money had hinted that he was on the verge of approaching the Missouri,

Kansas and Texas Railroad Company and telling them what a disgrace it was that they employed a chief of detectives who would not even honour his financial commitments.

The way the directors were viewing McKinley lately, that might be enough to cause them to dispense altogether with his services which, given the current state of his affairs, would be little short of a catastrophe.

There are however worse things than losing one's job and being pursued by a host of irate creditors and Bryan Bertram McKinley found that out the night he came to the last name on the list he had compiled of possible collaborators in his crooked scheme.

All in all, Parsons was a pretty respectable sort of town. Murders were few and far between and the commonest crimes were such trifling matters as stealing from shops and leaving hotels without paying the bill. It had been over a year since there had been a shooting in Parsons, and that had been a common or garden case of an angry husband chasing and killing a man when he'd come home unexpectedly and found his wife in bed with somebody else.

He had pursued and shot down the fellow and had been duly acquitted by a jury made up of men who would have done exactly the same thing had they found themselves in similar circumstances.

Be that as it might, that April there were some seriously unpleasant types crammed into the little town and since a number of them were professional killers it is perhaps not to be wondered at that something happened.

McKinley had been having a couple of drinks with each of those he was courting for his scheme and the natural consequence was that by the time he reached the final prospect the chief of detectives was far from sober. Not that this was noticeable; McKinley could hold his liquor as well as any man. But there can be no doubt at all that his judgement was impaired and this contributed greatly to what happened that night.

At half past nine in the evening McKinley tracked down the last name on his list of those in Parsons who were probably bounty hunters and might be in town on the way to the territories to look for the Vallence brothers. He was by this time tipsy, but not inebriated.

He had been directed to a little musical theatre which had recently opened. Perhaps calling the place a musical theatre was stretching it a bit, because as soon as he walked through the door he found himself in a hurdy-gurdy house, peopled by those who didn't mind paying for the company of pretty girls. This house was down a back street and McKinley had never even heard of it. He had to ask a dozen men before he could identify Paul Fitzgerald.

Having found the man he was looking for, McKinley went up and tapped him on the shoulder. Fitzgerald, a rawboned, red-headed Irishman, was deep in his cups and as soon as Mckinley touched the man's arm he knew that he had made a mistake. The Irishman whirled round and cried,

'Who laid a hand upon me? Let the man stand forth who dares to touch Paul Fitzgerald.'

This was a bad beginning and the detective was

more than half-minded to back out right that minute, except that one of Fitzgerald's companions pointed at McKinley and cried,

'Here's the man, Fitz! He's the one who grabbed you.'

'I didn't grab anybody,' said McKinley indignantly, to which Fitzgerald's response was immediate and uncompromising.

'Are ye saying my friend's a liar?'

'I think perhaps he got mixed up . . .' began McKinley, before the red-headed man in front of him roared,

'Mixed up, by God? I'll mix yourself up directly.'

'I did want to speak to you, Mr Fitzgerald. Perhaps we can go somewhere a little more private?'

Fitzgerald glanced round the smoky room, which was full of girls wearing skirts of a shortness that would have had them run in for indecency had they ventured out on to the public highway.

'This is private enough. What're you after, man?'

'I have a proposition for you. It's about the Vallence brothers. I hear you're looking for them.'

'Who are you?' asked the Irishman suspiciously, and it was now that McKinley made his great error. The noise in the hurdy-gurdy house was deafening, and even when you were shouting at the top of your voice the way that Paul Fitzgerald was, it was sometimes only possibly to catch half of what was being said. So when B.B. McKinley announced that he was the chief of detectives for the Missouri, Kansas and Texas Railroad Company, the only words that stood out to the intoxicated man he was trying to talk to were, *chief of detectives.*

'Detective are ye?' said Fitzgerald aggressively. 'I'm telling' ye now, the detective isn't born who can take Paul Fitzgerald in without losing some of his teeth and maybe his life in the process.'

Appalled, the chief of detectives started to say, 'No, no, Mr Fitzgerald, you got it all wrong.' He got no further than crying, 'No . . .' before the Irishman leaped at him.

Now McKinley had been in many rough houses and was quite capable of acquitting himself well in a fight, but he really didn't want to end up injuring this man, who looked to be his last hope of striking a deal that would enable him to get a share of the reward money for the Vallences. He did something which ran quite counter to his nature and was actually guaranteed to inflame the situation rather than calm it. He turned and ran.

With some men, as with a certain type of dog, showing fear, or the appearance of fear, is the very worst thing to do. As soon as McKinley fled Paul Fitzgerald gave chase, believing in his drunken haze that the man he had been speaking to was a detective on his trail. He was determined to find out what was going on and as the railroad detective ran from the hurdy-gurdy house into the street Paul Fitzgerald followed, stopping only to draw his pistol.

The two men ran down the narrow street, which eventually led to Parsons' main street. McKinley burst into the crowded thoroughfare, closely followed by Fitzgerald. If the latter had not been liquored up he most likely wouldn't have adopted the course of action that he then followed.

It consisted of firing a shot over the head of the man whom he took to be some cowardly wretch of a police officer who had been pestering him. He meant to fire a warning shot, but the state he was in made aiming impossible and he ended by shooting B.B. McKinley in the back.

Passers-by scattered in alarm at the sound of gunfire, some ducking into store doorways and others throwing themselves to the ground. It chanced that one of those passers-by, and incidentally the only man present who took no evasive action, was none other than Will Grafton, who, feeling restless, had decided to take a constitutional before turning in for the night.

He had recognized McKinley as the man came running towards him and had then been astonished to see him gunned down. He might not have liked the fellow over much, but he wasn't about to let somebody murder him like that in cold blood.

Paul Fitzgerald was standing in the middle of the road, with his gun in his hand. The sound of the shot he had fired and its effect of knocking the man he had been pursuing to the ground, had both had what one might not inaptly describe as a sobering effect upon the red-headed Irishman. He was probably ripe to be arrested by anybody who cared to attempt it, but that did not make the grocer's actions any less courageous.

Grafton reached into his pocket and pulled out the metal star which he had not yet chosen to wear. He pinned this to his jacket, pulled out the Smith &

Wesson and walked over to the man who had shot McKinley.

Then he said, 'You best come along with me to the sheriff's office. And just hand over that gun while you're about it.'

The befuddled man, aghast at what drink had caused him to do, saw the star on Grafton's jacket and the pistol in his hand and assumed quite naturally that he was being arrested. It has to be said that being arrested for foolish behaviour of this sort was anything other than a novelty for Paul Fitzgerald and he knew the rules well enough. He handed over his gun and allowed himself to be walked down to the sheriff's office which, mercifully, was still open.

The appearance of Will Grafton, sporting a deputy's star and holding a prisoner at gunpoint created a minor sensation. The deputy on duty had been on his way anyway to investigate the shot he had heard. He had delayed only to unlock the gun cabinet and select a Winchester. He had this in his hand when Grafton and Fitzgerald walked through the door.

Now although Grafton had explained his mission to the sheriff when he arrived in town, confiding in him that he had been deputized and carried warrants for the three Vallence brothers, the sheriff had not taken him very seriously and hadn't bothered to mention the business to his assistants. When Deputy Ike Stanmore saw Grafton's star he assumed that this was somebody who had just been engaged here in Parsons. This misunderstanding took some little time to resolve and when it had all been explained, Will Grafton went back to see if he could do anything for McKinley.

To his utter astonishment Grafton found that the detective was sitting up in the road and rubbing gingerly at his side.

'Mr McKinley, I never was so pleased to see anybody alive. I made sure you were dead.'

'Not yet, I ain't,' said the other. 'Bullet caught me in the ribs here, just grazed 'em, took all the skin off. Maybe one rib is cracked, but no more.'

'Well, I am pleased,' said Grafton. 'I have taken the man who shot you to the sheriff's office and he is locked in a cell.'

'You? You arrested that mad Irisher?'

'Indeed I did. He came quietly.'

McKinley stood up, wincing with the pain, then stuck out a hand to Will Grafton.

He said, 'I reckon I owe you for this. I thought I was going to die.'

The grocer was embarrassed and merely shrugged bashfully.

'You would have done the very same thing had the boot been on the other foot, I'm sure.'

'My cousin told me that you gave him a scare. You can believe that he wasn't commonly scared and yet you gave him a turn. I begin to see why.'

'Really, I'm not in that mould at all. I'm a grocer, nothing more. I told you my aim when first we met. I wish only to obtain justice. I'm not looking to oppose anybody else's interests.'

'I'm going to be honest with you, Mr Grafton . . .' began McKinley. He got no further before Will

Grafton told him gravely:

'It's often the best way.'

The detective couldn't make out whether or not this was said in deadly earnest or whether perhaps Grafton was having a little sober fun at his expense. Whichever it was, made no real odds. McKinley continued,

'I've not been altogether straight with you and what you did tonight makes me feel like a wretch. You saved my life and I owe you.'

'Not a bit of it,' protested Grafton. 'I did what I would for anybody. I don't need a reward.'

'I ain't talking of rewards. I'm talking about what's right. My job is to stop those Vallence boys in their tracks and you have precisely the very same aim. I can help you.'

Will Grafton could not have known it, but he was witnessing something little short of a miracle. It was many years since McKinley had undertaken any sort of action without an eye to the main chance. The first question he asked himself before he approached any enterprise was: *What's in it for me?*

Either coming so close to being killed had scrambled his brains, or the fear of death had awoken his conscience and made a better man of him. Whichever, he was offering to do something for another human being that not only would not benefit him in the slightest degree, but was actually liable to harm his own best interests. It was a remarkable moment indeed.

Perhaps Will Grafton was sensible of the magnitude of the offer being made to him, because he said gently,

'Mr McKinley, I'm not asking anything of you at all.'

'Ah, don't turn down my help, Mr Grafton. It's seldom enough I put myself out for others. Come, we'll work as team.'

'You mean that you don't have any objection to my trying to get those men back to California for trial?'

'Objection? Hell, I'll lend a hand escorting them, if it comes to that.'

'Well then, I am greatly obliged to you.'

This agreeable little scene was brought to an abrupt halt by the arrival of Courtney Adams, sheriff of Jackson County. He didn't look to be in a good frame of mind and was glaring angrily at Will Grafton.

CHAPTER 9

Sheriff Adams didn't look like a happy man as he walked up to McKinley and Grafton. He was staring at Grafton in particular in a way suggesting that he was not the world's biggest admirer of the grocer. He didn't waste any time at all in coming right to the point.

'Mr Grafton,' he said, 'when you fetched up here, you came to see me and explained that you had warrants for the arrest of all three of those Vallence boys. You also represented yourself to be a deputy sheriff. I wired Alila later and checked that out. You were telling the truth.'

'Of course I was telling the truth,' said Will Grafton. 'Why on earth would I make up a story like that?'

'You been in this job as long as me, you'd know that men lie about everything,' said Adams wearily. 'But that's nothing to the purpose. You might recall we also talked about your position here in Kansas and agreed that you had no powers of arrest nor anything like it?'

'Now that you mention it,' said Grafton slowly, 'I do remember some such discussion. But I've not come within a hundred miles of the men named in those warrants, so that don't signify.'

'Mr Grafton, don't fox with me. My deputy has a man locked up this minute who, he tells me, you delivered to him at gunpoint. Both he and the man you brought in thought you to be a deputy authorized by law to act here in Jackson County.'

'Oh, that. . . .' said Grafton thoughtfully.

'Yeah, that, Mr Grafton.'

'Truth to tell, I didn't really stop to think. Mr McKinley here had been shot and I thought it best to take steps to remove the gun from the man who shot him. After that, I took him straight to your office.'

'After first pinning a star to your jacket. Look, it's there now.'

'I thought,' said Will Grafton with disarming candour, 'that the fellow might take me more seriously if he thought I was a lawman.'

Sheriff Adams was torn between berating the man for putting it round that he was a duly authorized deputy of Jackson County and congratulating him for a smart piece of work. In the end, he compromised by saying,

'Well you brought him in all right, but don't make a habit of arresting people in this town, or I'm liable to get a little ticked off. You hear what I tell you?'

'I understand perfectly, Mr Adams, and I can assure you that it won't happen again.'

'Yes. In that case we'll say no more about it.' The sheriff turned to the chief of detectives from the railroad and said, 'I got a crow to pluck with you too, McKinley. Word is that you been doing your damnedest to recruit a bounty hunter. It won't answer in this town. Don't let me hear anything more of the sort.'

Having delivered himself of this final warning or piece of advice, Sheriff Adams turned on his heel and went back to his office.

Tom Vallence had been told by the Creek chieftain that the hunt for those who had carried out the latest attack on a train was all but over and that he and his brothers could leave as soon as they wished. Vallence tried to express his gratitude haltingly to the village leader, who merely grunted and turned his back. It was perfectly clear that the Creek had only been concealing the bandits because of the trouble they might cause white men in the future and not as an act of mercy.

The morning when they were to leave the vicinity of the Creek village Tom managed to sneak a few words alone with his brother Bob.

He said, 'I think the time is come to say 'bye to that Short fellow.'

Bob Vallence didn't at first apprehend his meaning and said,

'We got to sell that gold first an' divide up the proceeds.'

'No, I don't say so. We're goin' to bid him farewell afore we do so.'

It was then that Bob realized that his brother was going to kill Joe Short. There was a horrible kind of logic to it because, assuming they got anything like the going market rate for the gold, then Joe Short's share would come to around $500. Killing the man would be worth $500 to them and they had killed men for less than that in the past.

Short was already a little uneasy before the four of them had even left the Indian village. None of the brothers had spoken much to him and all their plans seemed to be predicated on just the three of them in the future.

Despite his unease, he didn't see how he could very well leave them before they had all got to Parsons and sold that gold. So he made a fatal error and ignored his fears, believing that the Vallences would hardly kill a man they had ridden with and who had played his part in all their recent activities. He could not have been more wrong.

The four riders picked their way along a path which wound round the back of the hills behind the Creek settlement and promised eventually to head north. They proceeded at a walk; the slope was treacherous, covered with loose scree. At length, the land levelled out and the men could carry on at a trot.

There was no conversation, which suited Joe Short just fine. After hardly having a word addressed to him all the time they had been in that damned cave, he was fed up with the brothers.

His only aim now was to collect his share of the money from the gold and then to strike out on his own. He had been doing all right until he picked up with the Vallences and could see no reason why he should not manage better in the future by his own self.

Short was considering his various options after leaving Parsons: which direction he should head, for instance, when Tom Vallence spurred his horse on until he was riding alongside Joe Short's right-hand side.

'All right there, Joe?' he enquired and then, quick as a rattlesnake, Vallence's hand shot out, plucked Short's pistol from its holster and flung it as far as he could.

'Hey, what the hell are you doing?' cried Short angrily. He prepared to canter off after his gun. He stopped because at that point Tom Vallence drew his own piece and aimed it straight at Short.

'What's to do?' asked Short, although deep down inside he must already have guessed how this was going to play out.

'Rein in,' said Vallence. Short did so. The other two brothers carried on for a space before they too halted. They were both of them a little more tender-hearted than Tom and both privately felt that it was a scurvy trick to shoot down somebody who had ridden with them.

Still and all, Tom was really in charge and neither Bob nor Pat were that fond of the fellow that they were inclined to interfere or set themselves up in opposition to Tom's intended action. Even so, they did not want to associate themselves with the murder and so salved their consciences by putting some physical distance between themselves and the act itself.

'What is this?' said Joe Short once more.

'What it is, is this,' explained Vallence in a sad voice, as though he truly regretted what was about to happen. 'We, which is to say me and my brothers, are moving on. You ain't needed any further.'

'You want I should go off alone?' asked Short, relief

flooding through him like a draught of whiskey. 'Sure thing, Tom. I'll go.'

'No, that ain't it. My brothers over yonder, they ain't worriers like me. It's like they trust folk. I don't. I'm always askin' myself things like, "What if such and such a man should be tempted to turn State's evidence against me?" or "What if this man or that might team up with a bounty killer and set him on my trail?" '

'Hell's a-fire, I ain't a-goin' to tell a soul anything. You can trust me.'

Tom Vallence shook his head. 'No, I can't. You want to say a prayer or aught of that kind and I'll hold off for a minute or two.'

'You goin' to shoot me down? You can't! You can't just kill me. It ain't right.'

'I know,' said Vallence understandingly. 'Life is cruel.' He fired twice into Short's chest without signalling his intention. Gazing into the man's eyes, the thing Tom Vallence most remarked was the look of tremendous surprise, like the fellow hadn't really believed right up to that last moment that Vallence was going to shoot him.

Joe Short's horse was well trained. It whinnied and jittered a little to one side, but otherwise was not spooked by the gunfire. Even when the rider slumped sideways and fell to the ground, one foot still tangled in one of the stirrups, the horse didn't shift. Tom Vallence dismounted and eased the dead man's foot from the stirrup. Then he began searching the corpse systematically.

Bob and Pat exchanged looks and Pat rolled his

eyes meaningfully. He and Bob were dyed-in-the-wool villains, but they surely had their limitations. Tom Vallence had none at all. Rifling through the belongings of a comrade he had just lately shot meant nothing at all to him.

He could have saved himself the trouble, because the dead man had nothing worth stealing. There were a few rounds of ammunition for his pistol, less than a dollar in loose coins, some tobacco and a rabbit's foot. He held this latter article up for his brothers' edification, saying,

'Lookee here, the damned fool was carrying a lucky rabbit's foot. It didn't bring him a heap of luck and that's a fact.'

Back in his hotel room, after the exciting events of that evening, Will Grafton was doing his best to work out whether he would do better to accept or reject the offer of help from B.B. McKinley. To put things bluntly, he didn't see that the detective would be much use to him, but at the same time he was touched by the man's attempt at restitution. It might be ungracious to refuse any assistance that McKinley was minded to give.

Really, he was more than glad to see the fellow turning away from the wrong path. He didn't of course know the full story, but he supposed that McKinley and his cousin had been intending to take the reward money for the Vallences and that this was more of a consideration to them than the administration of justice.

As he so often did when he was perplexed, Grafton sought the answer in prayer. He knelt at the side of the bed and said out loud,

'Dear Lord, guide me in this matter. I don't want to hurt Mr McKinley's feelings by turning down his offer and I think that he means well. If I reject his help, I'm afeared that he might take it as a snub and then fall back into his old ways again.'

By the time he climbed into bed, Will Grafton had made up his mind to continue on his own course, but to allow McKinley to think that he was helping.

It would have come as a great surprise to Will Grafton if he could have seen B.B. McKinley at the very moment that he himself was going to bed. He had formed the impression that Sheriff Adams and McKinley were next door to perfect strangers.

McKinley sat at a table in the kitchen of Sheriff Adams's house. Despite the remote and formal way that Adams and McKinley spoke to each other in public, they were actually fairly close acquaintances. It would not have been strictly accurate to describe them as friends, because the two men felt no special warmth towards each other. They were certainly not on such intimate terms that they were likely to be going out drinking together. It was more that their aims and concerns often coincided.

'Tell me straight, McKinley, what do you make to that fellow as pulled your chestnuts out of the fire tonight?' asked the sheriff.

'Really, I can't make him out at all. One minute you think he's soft as butter and the the next he's disarming a man I was running from in fear of my life. He's a strange one to figure.'

'I wasn't overly fussed when I heard that that mad cousin of yours had taken the train to the territories. It's nothing to me what shooting and killing takes place down there, but this town is another thing altogether.'

'What then? Jacob's dead; he ain't likely to trouble you now with his doings.'

Sheriff Adams looked long and hard at the chief of detectives for the Katy.

He said, 'It wasn't your cousin as I was thinking about now. What are you about, talking to a bunch of bounty hunters?'

'Ah, that's nothing. It's all finished with anyway.'

'What's finished with? I'll tell you my angle on this. I don't want any shooting in this town, nor any killing, robbing nor anything else. All those tricks are well and good south of the state line, but I don't want to see them here.'

'Adams,' said McKinley, 'my only hope now is to lend that grocer a hand in his quest, nothing more.'

'From all that I am able to collect, I would say he's more than able to paddle his own canoe without your help. Or mine either if it comes to it. You set mind to what I tell you now; I don't want any trouble here in town. See if you can take him south or something. I don't like him being here. He's the type that attracts trouble.'

'He's only a damned grocer, when all's said and done.'

'That's as maybe,' said Sheriff Adams. 'But I tell you now that I have from time to time come across men like him before. They're as polite as you like, butter won't melt in their mouth, but stuff happens around them. They act like lightning conductors. You know just what I'm talking about; you must have met such men yourself.'

'Happen so. But anyways, he saved my life this night. I owe him.'

While Will Grafton was getting into bed and B.B. McKinley and Sheriff Adams were talking in the sheriff's kithcen, the three Vallence brothers were sitting round a cheerful campfire, smoking and laying their plans for the next few days. Tom had kept his ideas secret until now, because he didn't want to share them with anybody other than his brothers, at least for the time being.

'I say we've finished with trains for a spell,' said Tom Vallence. 'I was hopeful that they'd bring us in a lot, but maybe I was wrong.'

'What then,' asked Pat. 'You got other ideas?'

'Yeah, that I have. I reckon you two are wanting somewhere to rest your heads for a bit. Not just a rock or a rolled-up pair of pants, like we got tonight, but a bed in a house of our own.'

Both Bob and Pat nodded their heads approvingly at this.

Bob said, 'There's a good deal in that. It'd be right nice to have a place of our own for a while.'

'This is how it stands,' Tom said. 'With luck, we'll

126

get two thousand for that gold. We need a man who won't ask too many questions, which'll drop the price some, but I won't take less than two thousand. That won't be enough to settle down. We'll need to buy a place with some land and we'll need stake money too, to tide us over 'til we get a regular business going.'

Pat interrupted at this point, saying, 'When you talk of business, you're meaning trading in horses and such, same as we talked about a few nights back?'

'Yeah, horses, cattle, anything as'll turn a quick profit. Word soon spreads about somewhere that buys horseflesh with no questions asked. We'll do well.'

Bob and Pat Vallence waited patiently to hear where they would be acquiring the rest of the funds needed to purchase this wonderful business opportunity. They knew that Tom didn't like to be badgered and pushed and that he would reveal in his own good time the course of action that he thought they should be following.

At last, after a silence which lasted a full three minutes, Tom spoke a again.

'There's two banks in Parsons. They are right prosperous and I propose that we hit the two of 'em, both on the same day.'

'Tom, how are we goin' to knock over two banks in one day, with just the three of us?' asked Pat. 'I don't see it at all.'

'It won't be just us,' said Tom. 'We're going to find another few men first.'

'Where? Here or in Parsons?'

'I'll warrant we come across some likely fellows

afore we reach the line. This territory's crawling with men on the scout. We keep heading north, you see, we'll come across somebody.'

Whether Tom Vallence was possessed of some fore-shadowing of the future, or maybe it was purely chance, the very next day saw the Vallence gang restored to a strength such as would enable them to hit the banks in Parsons.

The brothers rose at first light the next day and were soon on the trail. It was a fine day, although the red dawn gave notice that the weather could change for the worse later on. The three of them were all in good spirits and from time to time one or the other would sing a few verses of a song or whistle a cheery tune.

The terrain was rugged, but not arduous. There were gentle, undulating slopes coverd in loose rocks and cut across by little ravines and watercourses. From time to time they came upon steep hills which they found it more convenient to skirt around the side of. One such hill was like a miniature mountain, rearing up with rocky sides, the product of erosion by wind, rain and frost. As the three of them came around the side of this hill they suddenly found themselves con-fronted by three other riders.

The only thing that the encounter could possibly have been called was a confrontation, because the three riders swiftly spread out in a line, blocking the Vallence brothers' way forward. One thing that the brothers noted at once about the strangers was that they were all well dressed. The Vallences were dusty and dirty and all looked like they had been roughing it for weeks. By contrast, the three men facing them could just have walked out of a clothing store in a big city. They were immaculate.

Tom Vallence reined in and said in a voice soft with menace,

'Now then, what's all this here?'

One of the riders said, 'Good day to you. We're collecting for orphans and such and wondered if you might be able to spare some of your riches.' This was said amiably enough, but it was as plain as could be that this was a hold-up. Tom Vallence shook his head very slowly. He said:

'You boys want to back off right this second and move aside, we'll let you go. You carry on down this road though and before God, the three of you are as good as dead. You picked the wrong men to fool with, you'll see.'

'Well, that's straight enough talking,' said the man who had accosted them. His hand moved a mite too quickly for Tom Vallence's liking and, although he could just have been shaking the reins with a view to moving out of the way, Vallence took the gesture to be indicative of a man about to go for his gun.

He drew at once and his two brothers were no more than a split second behind him. In short order, the three strangers also drew and the two parties sat there on their horses, drawing down on each other, with neither group looking like it was going to back down.

The man who had first spoken to them smiled broadly and said,

'Shall we let the bugles sing truce?' So saying he replaced his gun in its holster and signalled that his two companions should do likewise. Then he said, 'I've a notion that I'm addressing the infamous brothers Vallence. Is that so?'

'What's it to you?' asked Tom, still with his pistol pointing straight at the man. Bob and Pat also kept their guns trained on the other men, at least until they knew what the game was.

'It's this,' said the man. 'My name's Carol and me and my friends are, as you might say, on the scout. We're looking for some bigger fish than we've been able to find. Heard about you boys and your exploits, of course. What say we set down and talk about things as might be to our mutual advantage.'

'What the hell kind of name is Carol for a man?' asked Tom. 'I never heard the like. And how come you talk so fancy?'

One of the strangers laughed at this and explained, 'It comes of having an education. Carol here is a college man. He's fallen into bad ways since then, though, as you can see.'

Tom Vallence was torn between irritation at the way that these men spoke, like they were superior to him, and by his need for another three or four men if he was to have a realistic chance of taking the banks in Parsons. He said,

'I don't see what's in it for us, teaming up with a set of dandies like you fellows. You sure our rough ways wouldn't put you out none?'

130

CHAPTER 10

Will Grafton was certain sure that they could expect the Vallence brothers to be passing through Parsons, and probably halting for while, within the next three or four days. He had explained his reasoning to McKinley and the chief of detectives was compelled to agree that it was a sound enough theory.

'Mind,' he said, 'you can't always tell what boys like that will be up to or do next. You think you have 'em pegged and then they plumb surprise you.'

'Well, that's true enough,' said Grafton. 'But if I'm wrong the worst I do is waste a few more days. I won't deny I'm awful anxious about my store and raring to get back to it, but having set out on this track, I reckon I'll stick with it to the finish.'

'What'll you do if the Vallences show up here?' asked McKinley curiously. 'There's apt to be at least three of them, plus whatever hangers on they carrying along with them.'

Will Grafton scratched his head and said, 'Do you know, Mr McKinley, I haven't given that a right lot of thought. I suppose I will show them the warrants and ask them to accompany me back to Alila.'

'You got a hard row to hoe there and no mistake. Like as not they'll draw on you.'

'Ah, Mr McKinley, the good Christian does not flinch from difficulties. I never thought that catching those men would be a walk in the park.'

'You want that I should help you arrest them? You mind, though, what the sheriff said last night about not wanting to see any arrests made in this town without his say-so.'

The grocer laughed. 'I hadn't forgot that. Sometimes though, you have to follow a higher law than that of man.'

'I wouldn't let Adams hear you saying so,' muttered McKinley.

When he got up that morning, Grafton had felt very sad. He'd been dreaming about Carrie and he also missed his children. Although B.B. McKinley was not the type of man whom Will Grafton would in the normal way of things be spending much time with, Garfton found that just talking with another being was raising his spirits and making him cheer up. He had no doubt at all that for all that he was chief of detectives, McKinley was a bit of a rogue, but even so, his companionship was not disagreeable. All in all, he was glad that he had decided last night to accept the man's offer of help.

The six men were sitting smoking in the lee of this hill which just recently had looked certain to be the scene of a bloody gun battle. The three fellows, Carol, Rod and Marcus had until a week or so back been employed in a travelling show. They were crack shots who had astounded the audience with their tricks in the arena. There had been some species of argument with the man running the show and, as a consequence, they had parted company in Arkansas and come into the territories. They had soon found that there was money to be made robbing other travellers and were working their way through until something else came up. Their ultimate ambition appeared to be to set up their own show: something to rival Bill Cody.

'So how good are you fellows?' asked Tom Vallence. 'You sure your shooting ain't a load of tricks? I seen such things, you know.'

'Tricks?' said Carol, in mock indignation. 'Tricks? I don't think so. One of you boys want to volunteer to be my target?'

There were no takers among the Vallences and so the man called Rod stood up. He went over to the saddle-bag on his horse and came back with a clay pipe and a silver table knife with an exceedingly shiny blade. He handed the knife to Carol and the clay pipe to Tom, saying,

'Best examine it and see that there's nothing rummy about it.'

Tom Vallence and his brothers having satisfied themselves that the clay pipe was the genuine article, they handed it back to Rod, who popped it in his mouth and then walked off to a distance of twenty yards or so.

Pat observed, 'I could do what they're doing so far, twenty-five yards ain't nothing.'

'Ah, but now watch,' said Carol. He drew his pistol. This was a shiny, nickel-plated forty-five. He stood with his back to the man with the clay pipe in his mouth and then held the blade of the knife in front of his face. Having turned so that the reflection was clear, he aimed over his shoulder and with scarcely a pause, fired at Rod, shattering the clay pipe as it rested between his lips.

'God almighty,' breathed Bob Vallence. 'I never saw the like.'

'Can you all shoot so?' asked Tom.

'Well now,' replied Carol, 'Rod is better than any of us with a rifle. Rod, fetch your piece.'

When the other man had pulled a handsome-looking rifle out of a scabbard at the front of his saddle, Carol said,

'Any of you men got such a thing as an egg? No?' He went and rummaged around in his own bag and produced a ball of clay, no larger than a hen's egg. 'It's more impressive with a real egg, makes more mess, but this will give you the idea.'

Rod was standing completely at his ease, the rifle held carelessly in his hands. When Carol threw the ball into the air he looked up in apparent surprise, then worked the lever and fired once. The ball was blown to atoms.

'I'll allow you fellows can shoot,' said Tom, in reluctant admiration. 'But are you ready to kill men as well?'

'If need be,' said Carol. 'It's nothing to us. You want that we should work together for a spell, then we're game.'

'You got yourselves a deal,' said Tom Vallence casually, concealing his delight at their good fortune in picking up with such useful men. He had no doubt that between the six of them, they would be able to take out those banks in Parsons and be back on the road in next to no time at all.

Sheriff Adams chanced across Grafton and McKinley, as the two of them strolled down Main Street that morning. He said to McKinley,

'That Irisher's sobered up now and swearing that he meant you no harm. Says his gun went off by accident. What do you say, you want to prosecute or not?'

'Hell, no,' said McKinley. 'It's the sort of misunderstanding as could happen to any of us. Don't keep a-hold of him on my account.'

Adams turned to Will Grafton and said, 'I'm mighty pleased to see that you're not wearing that star this morning, Mr Grafton. You won't think me rude if I ask what you're still hanging round this town for?'

'Oh, I don't believe that I'll be here above another five days, Sheriff. Say a week at the outside. I'm just enjoying a holiday now, nothing more.'

Sheriff Adams stared at Grafton suspiciously. 'I won't deceive you, Mr Grafton, we don't get all that many tourists coming here. Thomas Cook and Sons ain't yet included Parsons on their itinerary and I'd take oath that you are the only man currently in town who says he's here for a holiday.'

McKinley cut in at this point, saying, 'Hey, we're only taking a rest here, you know. Nobody's going to cause you any problems.'

Adams went off feeling far from easy in his own mind about things. There was nothing he could put his finger upon, but that combination of McKinley and the man from California didn't sit well with the sheriff. Grafton might be persuaded that B.B. McKinley had somehow had a religious revelation or something and was now going to be helping his fellow man for the sake of it, but Sheriff Adams didn't believe a word of it. He could not imagine McKinley involving himself in any affair unless there was a strong business end in it for him.

After the sheriff had left them, Will Grafton said,

'Tell me, Mr McKinley, where would you go if you had some stolen precious metals to dispose of?'

'Depends.'

'On what?'

'On whether I was after a quick sale, or if I was ready to dicker and get a better price.'

'I can't see those Vallence brothers settling for anything other than the market rate, can you?'

McKinley thought about this for a bit, then said, 'I think you're right. They gone to a deal of trouble getting hold of that gold. They all goin' to hang if they're caught and they know it. They'll want full value for their money.'

'So where would you go, if you were to sell it here in Parsons?'

'There's a little shop, down the way a bit. Buys and sells 'most anything, but 'specially jewellery. Fellow as runs it, name of Hartmann, he's got all manner of contacts and can unload things to others.'

'You think he'd be in the market for stolen ingots of gold?'

'I think,' said McKinley, 'he'd be in the market for selling his own grandmother's skin to cover furniture with, if the price was right.'

'We got two bits of business in Parsons,' Tom Vallence said to the man who went by the strange name of Carol. 'One ain't any o' your concern. The other is robbin' banks. You want in?'

'Oh yes, we want in all right. But only if the terms are good.'

'What's that mean?'

'Means we hear all sorts of stories.'

'Come on,' said Tom, 'out with it. Don't go tiptoeing round the ranch. What d'you mean?'

'It's easy enough. Men who ride with you and your brothers look to have a short life expectancy. We'll team up with you for raiding those banks, but we divide up the money in this way. You take all the proceeds from one bank and we'll take all from another.'

This proposal was so unusual that it took Tom back a little. Neither of his brothers knew what to make of it either. The tradition in such enterprises was to pool the money and then divide it by the number of men who had taken part in the raid.

Tom Vallence said, 'Don't you trust me and my

brothers to play fair?'

'It's not that,' said Carol. 'After a raid on two banks it would madness for all six of us to ride off together. There'll be posses and men from every vigilance committee in Kansas hunting for us. Much better to split up. I don't want that we should sit down after the robberies and then start going, 'One for you, one for me' and so on.'

'That the only reason?'

'Pretty well, apart from where you and your brothers have had a number of partners, from what we heard. Where are they all now?'

Neither Tom nor his brothers said anything to that, so Carol continued pleasantly,

'You see what I mean? The members of your gang don't seem to be around for the shareout. We don't want to end up as more of those unfortunate cases.'

Tom was greatly minded to tell these tailors' dummies to get lost and tend to their own affairs. Problem was that he really needed some more guns. There could not be the least doubt that these fellows could shoot straight. He said, 'You got yourself a deal. Only, us boys get first pick; we choose which bank's money we take.'

'Yes, we can do that,' said Carol. 'I mind that both those banks in Parsons will have plenty for us.' He leaned forward and offered his hand to Tom Vallence, who took it. They shook.

Hartmann's shop was on Main Street, but you could walk past it without even noticing it. There was no sign

138

over it, nor any window on to the sidewalk, and it wasn't until you walked through the door that you could even tell what the proprietor was trading in. Around the walls were glass cabinets full of clocks, vases, fine porcelain, sets of cutlery, and anything else that was both portable and valuable.

Hartmann himself sat behind a glass counter, beneath which were watches, cufflinks and jewellery. When Grafton and McKinley entered, the owner of the store barked rudely at them,

'Yes, what is it? What are you after?' He had an accent that Will Grafton took to be German.

'Let me do the talking,' said McKinley softly. 'I know how he operates.' Then more loudly, he said, 'Good morning, Mr Hartmann. I wonder if you could help me. I'm looking to sell some gold.'

'Yes, yes. How much?'

'What are you offering an ounce?'

'Depends what it is. Jewellery? Nuggets?'

'Say it was nuggets. Just pure gold. How much?'

'More than an ounce? More than five ounces?'

'More than five ounces.'

'Twenty dollars an ounce. Take it or leave it. Show me.'

'I got to go and fetch it.'

'Ach, you waste my time. Get out. Don't come back unless you have goods with you.'

Outside the store McKinley said, 'He's the man, for a bet. Five times sixteen is . . . what?'

'Eighty,' replied Will Grafton at once. 'Times twenty makes sixteen hundred. The Vallences aren't going to retire rich on that.'

'No, I'd say you're right there. Still, you can be sure they'll end up at Hartmann's when they do come to town.' McKinley looked up at the neighbouring buildings. 'If you're right about those boys heading this way, and I don't say you are or you ain't, you can bet they'll be walking through that door at some point. I reckon we could do a sight worse than stake out Hartmann's and watch who goes in and out.'

'As far as it goes, that's a sound idea. The only thing that strikes me is that I don't have the least notion what any of those men look like, excepting what I read in the newspapers. What about you?'

'No, I got no more than you. Just the descriptions published, which is mostly a lot of foolishness. 'Fresh complected, even features, average height', that kind of thing.'

'What on earth are "even features"?' asked Will Grafton. 'Don't we all have even features?'

'Like I say, it's all nonsense. We'll have to find some way to identify them.'

The Vallences and their new partners were only twenty miles or so from Parsons. They did not intend to enter the town that night, even if they got there before dusk. The reason was simple. Nobody had any clear description of the brothers and there were no photographs circulating. The less time they spent in the town of Parsons, the less chance there would be later of some smart person coming forward with a detailed and accurate description of them.

The same thing was a worry for the former circus troupe, only even more so. At least the Vallences might pass for travel-stained saddle-tramps, but nobody could say the same of the sharpshooters: they stuck out a mile. Anybody setting eyes on those three would be sure to recall them later.

As they trotted along Carol said to nobody in particular,

'We might need disguises. I have the very thing, right here in my bag.'

'You're a regular marvel, you know that, Carol?' said Tom sarcastically. 'Always thinking of stuff we poor fools would never have given a thought to. Only in this case, we got disguises already. We call 'em masks.'

'Oh, but you just draw attention to yourself with those,' said Carol, laughing, 'I've a far better idea and it's worked for us.'

'Well then, we don't need any new ideas.'

Pat Vallence said. 'Ah, let him show us what he's got in mind, Tom. It ain't goin' to hurt.'

'Go on then,' said Tom. 'Let's see what you use.'

Carol said, 'We worked with a theatre for a space; it used to run alongside our show. We took some of their properties, what they call "props".'

'Anybody ever tell you as you talk a lot, Carol?' asked Tom Vallence. 'Or that you're a damned show-off?'

'It might have been mentioned once or twice,' admitted the other. He took out what Tom took at first to be a bunch of dead animals: cats or raccoons or some such. Then he saw that the objects were in fact

141

false beards. He was secretly impressed, but had no intention of letting the sharpshooters see it. He said grudgingly:

'I suppose they might answer.'

Pat Vallence was tickled at the thought of wearing false beards. He said to Carol, 'Hey, can I try one o' them things?'

'Of course. Help yourself.'

The others fell about laughing at the comical sight of Pat Vallence wearing a long, black beard. Bob and Tom didn't want to be left out and they too tried on the beards. The things were actually quite realistic, the only giveaway being that they had to be hooked over the ears.

Carol said, 'We have a little bottle of spirit gum to attach them to your cheeks. They will look all right, trust me.'

'We goin' to look like those Bible-bashers,' said Pat. 'You know, those foreigners who don't never shave theyselves. There's nobody at all will recognize us wearing these, never mind be able to give a good description when we dig up.'

'Listen,' said Carol to Tom. 'Is the aim to take those banks one after another or both at the same time?'

'One after the other. If only three of us go into a bank, then there's always some clever bastard as'll try and be a hero. They're less apt to do that when there's a whole bunch of men.'

The man called Marcus said, 'It'll be quick work though, robbing one bank and then scooting off to do another.'

'They're both on Main Street,' said Tom Vallence. 'Not fifty yards apart, although on opposite sides of the street. We move fast enough and shoot up the place a bit, it's goin' to be fine. Whole thing won't take more than ten minutes to accomplish.'

For the rest of the day the six riders carried on north towards Parsons. Although the three men from the circus act were a little snotty, they were lively enough company and even Tom began to feel cheerful and easy with them. They were certainly a cut above some of those whom they had picked up with lately.

'It's a toss-up,' said McKinley, 'between we stake out Hartmann's store and watch who comes in and out, or we set a watch on the road south into the territories.'

'What would you do, Mr McKinley? If this was some operation that you were overseeing?'

'Problem is, Mr Grafton, those boys most likely won't ride straight in from the south. If I were them, I'd circle round and maybe one come from one way and a couple more from the opposite side of town. Stands to reason that a body of men entering here from the south all at one go might jog folk's memories about the recent robberies.

'I'd say that we should have one of us on a roof overlooking Hartmann's and another walking up and down Main Street, looking out for men who look like they been living rough. We know we're looking for men in their early twenties.'

'I think that all sounds about right. Shall we meet tomorrow morning and start our observations?'

143

'Yes, that might do well enough. I'll level with you: my own bosses are getting restless about this as well. I'm guessing that if you were to take them back to California to stand trial for that affair at Alila, that would suit the Southern Pacific. Since they're joined together with the Katy in this reward business, I suppose that might be agreeable to all parties.'

'I hope,' said Will Grafton sincerely, 'that I'm not putting you out by any of this?'

'Don't you fret none about that. I pay my debts, Mr Grafton. Long as you need my help, you got it.'

CHAPTER 11

The poor weather that had threatened at dawn the previous day arrived in strength during the night. A storm swept in from the west, which left the six men camped outside Parsons feeling pretty cold and miserable. Sleeping in the open is one thing when the weather's fine; it's quite another when you're lying down in the pouring rain.

The six men couldn't sleep and so were up, stamping about and trying to keep up their spirits, at about an hour before the first glimmer of dawn. Carol and his men were the more annoyed, being concerned at the mud on their fine clothes. Since the Vallences were all over dirt and mud already, this was not a matter of such concern to them.

Tom Valence had an idea that the three dandies, as he thought of them, were bothered about their fancy rigs because they were hoping to hire themselves out again as a troop of sharpshooters at a carnival or circus. Those boys were not, he guessed, aiming to make a career of banditry, but rather hoping to raise a little stake money by a few easy robberies.

'Can't we just get moving?' asked Carol. 'This rain will be the death of me.'

'It'll be the death of us if we march into Parsons before dawn, when there's not a living soul to be seen on the streets,' replied Tom Vallence emphatically. 'It will purely invite attention. No, we stay here until I gauge there'll be folk moving about and we can lose ourselves in the crowd.'

The Vallences didn't like standing around while the cold rain lashed them any more than the circus men did, but they knew that there were worse things than having water running down the back of your neck. Things like being caught for a string of murders and being hanged, for example.

'Can't we least move where we might get a mite more shelter from this cursed rain?' asked Rod.

'No. We stay right where we are,' said Tom. 'We can't be seen from town here and I don't want anybody looking out their windows and seeing a half-dozen men prowling round and making no attempt to get out o' the rain. It'll look downright suspicious. Stop complaining.'

So it was that for the next two hours the six men walked up and down by their horses, unable to smoke and with barely anything to eat. By the time it was light they were not in the best of moods, to say the very least of it.

When Will Grafton woke up that morning he was certain for a moment that he had heard his wife's voice. As he first came to, he didn't remember that she was dead, but thought drowsily that Carrie had just got up and spoken to him as she left the room. Then the events of the last few weeks came flooding back and he experienced again that sharp pain of separation; the desolation of knowing that the person he loved most in all the world had been snatched away from him.

He lay there for a while, mulling things over in his mind. He supposed that what he had taken to be Carrie's voice was the echo of a dream that he must have had. Even so, he racked his brains, trying to recall what she had said, as though he had been vouchsafed a last message from beyond the grave.

Then Grafton recollected what scripture had to say about such matters and he knew that there had been no particular significance to his dream, that his beloved wife was walking the streets of glory now and not drifting down to earth to whisper in a sleeping man's ear.

Grafton got out of bed and splashed cold water over his face from the pitcher on the washstand. It might be an important day today and he wanted his mind to be clear and sharp, not filled up with a lot of foolishness about ghosts and suchlike.

It was nine when the grocer went down to have breakfast in the eating house across the street. He was pleasantly surprised to find that the chief of detectives for the railroad was already there, sipping a cup of coffee. He greeted Grafton in a jocular vein, saying,

'Lord, I thought you Christians were supposed to be early risers, but you are a real slug-a-bed. Don't it say something in the Bible about "Go to the ant, thou sluggard, consider her ways and be wise"?'

'Didn't think you were a one for scripture, Mr McKinley. Or so I apprehended from what you said the other day.'

'Ah, well, my mother was. Sent me to church regular and made me read the good book. Some of it can't help but seep in.'

'The weather is pretty dreadful this morning,' said Grafton. 'Looking at that sky, I doubt the rain will ease off before midday. If you like, I'll take first watch on the roof, while you look round the streets.'

'You really are a Christian, offering to sit up there on the roof on a morning like this,' said McKinley, joshing, but at the same time with a note of real admiration in his voice. 'All right, I won't argue with you.'

After breakfast the two men walked round to the alley behind the line of buildings opposite Hartmann's store. A fire escape led up to the windows at the back of the buildings and continued right up to the rooftop.

'You know,' said McKinley, 'I got a rifle back at my place that you could have up here. If things start down in the street, you would be well placed up here to join in the action without risking yourself overmuch.'

Will Grafton gave the detective a strange look.

'I'm sure that the offer is kindly meant, Mr McKinley,' he said, 'but really, it isn't to be thought of. I can't go firing down through this rain at various people who I think might be up to no good. Apart from it being downright cowardly to take a man like that without first challenging and defying him, it's a perfect recipe for killing an innocent passer-by. No, if anything begins, I'll just come down those stairs and join in.'

'I'll say this for you, Mr Grafton, you don't want for courage.'

'It's not that at all,' said the grocer, laughing apologetically. 'Courage don't enter into the equation. I'm as scared of death as the next man. It's what's right and wrong that concerns me. If I'm going to die, I'd as soon a-do so with a clear conscience.'

'Well, you beat all. That's all I can say about the subject. I'll be back up here if I see anything worthy of our attention.'

If anything the rain was getting heavier as the six riders picked their way through the mud into Parsons. Just as B.B. McKinley had suggested, the group had split up: three were entering the town from the north and the other half of the party from the west. It had been agreed that they would meet up in Main Street.

Tom Vallence had come to a decision about the gold, which he had not yet mentioned to his brothers, and that was that he wasn't going to waste any time, after all, selling it in Parsons. If their assaults on the banks went according to plan, then they would have plenty of cash money to tide them over, in which case the gold could act as their reserve.

His face was itching and tickling with the false beard. The rain didn't help matters, plastering the hair against his mouth and nose. Tom had to admit though, these beards beat the neckerchiefs when it came to disguising themselves. Here they were, entering town now and looking so that their own mother wouldn't know them, but at the same time not drawing the frightened looks that masks would be sure to do.

'We ain't selling the gold in this here town,' said Tom to his brothers, as they turned into Main Street. 'I want that we should simply take them banks and go.'

'Just like you say, Tom,' said his brother Bob. 'You know best.'

Ahead, they saw Carol, Rod and Marcus; dawdling along in the same direction and looking like they were no more than travellers who'd just fetched up in town and didn't know where they would go next. There was nothing at all about either of the groups of three men that would arouse the slightest suspicion in anyone.

Fifty yards down the road was the imposing, brick-built edifice of the First National Bank of Kansas. It was the smartest building in the whole town, with a triangular pediment at the front of the roof and brightly painted white window frames, with storm shutters. It was also a half-mile from Hartmann's store, which meant that the robbers would not even pass by that section of Main Street that Will Grafton was so carefully watching.

Now the best-laid plans in the world, whether those plans have been laid by good men or bad, can be over-turned and set at naught by some trifling incident that nobody could have foreseen. That is precisely what happened that rainy and overcast morning in Parsons.

The driver of the train who had been threatened

with death by Bob Vallence had been given a little vacation by his bosses at the Missouri, Kansas and Texas Railroad Company. He had been told that he could spend two weeks on full pay just taking it easy and not working. The directors at the Katy thought this a nice gesture towards a man who had nearly been killed.

Since Jack Renton, the driver, had a relative in Parsons, he had chosen to take a few days resting there to see his daughter and her family.

Renton was hurrying along through the driving rain, his head down and aiming only to get to the store to do a little shopping for his daughter. Because he wasn't looking where he was going, he actually bumped right into a man standing on the sidewalk outside the bank.

Maybe the bank had opened late, because when he looked up Renton had the idea that the man into whom he had barged formed part of a line outside the doors of the bank. He looked into the fellow's face to apologize for his clumsiness and for not looking where he was going, and found himself staring at the very man who had offered to shoot him only a few days previously.

True, he hadn't had a thick black beard then, but you don't tend to forget the eyes of somebody who is drawing down on you like that. There was not the least doubt in Jack Renton's mind that this was one of the Vallence brothers who had robbed the passengers on his train. Mumbling an inarticulate apology, Renton moved off, hearing one of the men say irritably,

'Clumsy cowson.'

At first the driver didn't know what to do. Then it came to him that the best course of action would be to raise the alarm as widely as possible. He walked into the middle of the street, dodging horses and causing the driver of a cart to curse him, and then shouted at the top of his voice:

'The Vallences are here! The Vallence brothers are over there, robbing the bank.'

At first, passers-by looked curiously at the man who was standing there in the rain, yelling about the Vallence brothers. Then some looked towards the bank, where a huddle of men were standing. All had luxuriant black beards and now had pistols in their hands as well. They were looking round angrily, to see who was shouting about them.

Then somebody else took up the cry. 'The Vallences are robbing the bank!'

So heavy was the rain and such a racket did it make, bouncing off the roof, that Will Grafton didn't hear the shouting down in the road. He was focusing his attention on the door to Hartmann's store. Then there came the distinctive and quite unmistakable sound of gunfire. It came from Grafton's right and he peered through the curtain of rain to see if he could make out what was happening.

It did not take him long to decide that it was too much of a coincidence that he was watching out for a set of outlaws and now there was shooting on Main Street. He stood up and made his way down the steps leading to the alley.

The role played by McKinley that day was brief and inglorious. He heard the shouts announcing the name of the Vallences and ran at once in that direction. Those standing on the sidewalk across from the bank were staring and pointing and McKinley saw the strange-looking bunch of men huddled by the door of the bank.

He drew his piece and without shouting any sort of warning or challenge, began firing at the men. He got off two shots, one of which hit Bob Vallence in the shoulder, and he was preparing to gun down as many as he could before they realized where the fire was coming from, when he received a great shock.

The circus man called Rod was standing just ten feet from him and he was carrying his rifle, wrapped up in an oilskin slicker to protect it from the rain. He had been positioned over there as a backstop, to take out any lawmen who might arrive while the others were in the bank. Rod simply raised his gun and shot McKinley down where he stood, the bullet passing right through the detective's ear.

The sharpshooter turned his attention once more to the bank, then fell himself as Sheriff Adams came running up, his pistol already drawn. He saw McKinley's death and without hesitating shot down the man with the rifle.

Across the road it was very clear to the five men clustered in the porch of the bank that they were not going to be able to rob even one bank, never mind two. Those people who had no personal involvement in the developing gun battle began to run for cover or dive into the nearby stores. Women were screaming and men shouting oaths.

Adams was hoping that his deputies would have the sense to bring rifles or scatterguns when they eventually bestirred themselves and came to join the party. Then his eyes fell upon the Winchester dropped by the man he had killed. He bent down, picked it up and worked another round into the chamber.

It wasn't hard for Grafton to tell where the centre of the disturbance was as he approached the bank building. He could see people fleeing in terror and hear the cries of distress. There appeared to be four or five men on the sidewalk ahead and another slumped near by. Since these men were not reacting in any way to the gunfire, it was a fair bet that they were somehow mixed up with it.

Grafton drew the Smith & Wesson from inside his jacket and moved forwards until he could be sure that the men were up to no good. As he got a little closer, he saw that all four of those standing there had pistols in their hands, and that clinched it for him. He ducked into the doorway of a store a couple of buildings along from the bank, then leaned his head out and shouted through the driving rain,

'Throw down your weapons!'

Sheriff Adams heard Will Grafton calling upon the men to surrender and his face contorted in fury. He thought that he had made his views on all that sort of carry-on quite clear. Adams was crouched in a doorway with a good view of the bank and, with the rifle he had trained on them, he could easily have shot them all.

He was not a man who liked to take life needlessly, though, and he was still hoping that he might be able to talk the men into laying down their guns. Grafton was going to queer that pitch for him if he carried on.

One of the men by the bank fired down the street when he heard the grocer shouting and Sheriff Adams came to the conclusion that he couldn't take a chance on bullets flying up and down Main Street like that. He took careful aim and' shot one of the would-be bank robbers.

Then the very thing that he had feared occurred: the group split into two. Two men ran off down the street and one dragged the wounded man into the bank and closed the door behind them.

It was a close call, but Adams figured that the two running men were more likely to cause mischief than the two holed up in the bank, so he gave chase, cursing his deputies and wondering where in the hell they had got to.

'I'm hurting real bad, Tom,' said Bob Vallence. 'I reckon as that ball broke my collar bone.' He was lying on the carpeted floor of the bank. A small huddle of terrified customers cowered against the wall, as far as they could possibly get from the grim-faced men by the door.

'You'll be fine,' Tom told his brother. 'Just lie still now.' Through the glass panel in the door he saw the man who had been firing at them go haring off up the road after Carol and Marcus.

'Where's Pat?'

'He's dead,' said Tom. 'Bullet took him straight in the chest.'

'That's the hell of a thing.'

'Ain't it, though? Can you get on to your horse, if'n I help you up?'

'Well, I can sure as hell try,' said Bob Vallence, smiling gamely through the agonizing pain of a shattered collar bone. 'You want we should make a run for it now?'

Tom Vallence was crouching by the street door of the bank, his pistol in his hand. He peered through the glass, established that the street was deserted and said,

'Yeah, let's make tracks.' As he spoke the door was kicked open, knocking the gun from Tom's hand. Before he had time to dive for it a figure appeared in the doorway. This insignificant and colourless-looking man had in his hand a short barrelled revolver.

He said to Tom Vallence, 'I'm strongly of the opinion that you are two of the Vallence brothers.'

'You got that right,' said Tom Vallence. 'But who are you?'

'Me? I'm nobody. Just a grocer from Alila in California. You men killed my wife and I've come to call you to account for it.'

Tom Vallence had never been much of a one for long and convoluted conversations. It was enough for him to know that this man was hoping to prevent his escape. He hurled himself across the floor in pursuit of his gun. His fingers had just closed upon the hilt of the weapon when the first bullet hit him in the side. It felt like he'd been kicked in the ribs, but he still tried to bring up the pistol, stopping only when another bullet took him full in the chest and burst open his heart.

Seeing this stranger gun down his favourite brother, Bob Vallence tried to pull his pistol from its holster with his left hand, his right being useless on account of the broken collar bone. Seeing the movement, Will Grafton turned and shot the wounded man in the chest.

When Sheriff Adams returned from the brief but deadly gun battle, in the course of which he and his deputies had killed the remaining members of the gang, he found Will Grafton in charge of the bank, comforting a pair of hysterical women. Just inside the door were two corpses. The clerks and other customers of the First National Bank could not speak too highly of the man who had rescued them, as they believed, from certain death at the hands of the Vallence gang.

CHAPTER 12

Martha brought the children to the depot to meet the train bringing their father home. She could scarcely expect them to go to school on such a day. Each day, the children asked the same question: 'Do you think Pa will come home today?' and every day she had been obliged to answer that she didn't know.

Billy-Joe had at first evinced a slight reluctance to come to the depot with her, because he could not rid his mind of the terrible scene that he had witnessed there, when his mother was killed right in front of him. His aunt, though, assured him that he needed to confront such fears and not give way to them.

It was Martha who first caught sight of Will Grafton. She was immensely relieved to see that he looked much the same as usual: a unremarkable, slightly fussy-looking little middle-aged man, with receding hair and steel-rimmed eyeglasses. He looked every inch a grocer.

'Martha,' said her brother when he saw her, 'it surely is good to see you again. I hope these children of mine haven't been leading you a dance?'

He smiled at the three children when he said this, to show that he was only joking and that in reality he was confident that they had all behaved well for their aunt. Then he opened his arms and the three of them rushed to him. He returned their hugs so fiercely that little Ella complained that she was being crushed to death.

As they walked home both Billy-Joe and Linton were eager to hear about what had become of the bad men who hurt their mama, but Grafton was strangely reticent about the subject.

'But Pa,' said Billy-Joe, 'what became of the men?'

'Why now,' replied his father, 'I'm sorry to say that they died.' His sister shot him a startled glance on hearing this intelligence.

'What did they die of?' asked Linton. 'Were they sick?'

'That's one way of setting out the case, son. Those fellows lived such a life, they were bound to come to a bad end, and that sooner rather than later. If you boys spent as much time studying scripture as you do reading dime novels, you'd maybe have read where the good book tells us that all them as live by the sword, die by the sword.'

Billy-Joe said, 'Frank Springer at school says that his father told him he sold you a gun before you went. Is is true?'

'Yes, it's true enough. Why do you ask?'

'Oh, nothing,' said his son, a little bashfully. 'It's just that . . . well, I'd sure like to see it.'

'I'm real sorry son,' his father told him, 'but I got rid of it while I was away.'

'Ah shucks,' said Billy-Joe. 'Why'd you do that, sir?'

Will Grafton stretched his arm out and threw it around the shoulders of his elder son.

'Why? 'Cause I'm a grocer, son. What in tarnation would I be needing a gun for?'

As they approached the white-painted clapboard house Will Grafton stopped dead for a second and stared at the place, like it was the best thing he'd ever seen in his life.

Then he said, 'It sure is good to be home.'